The Blue
Geography

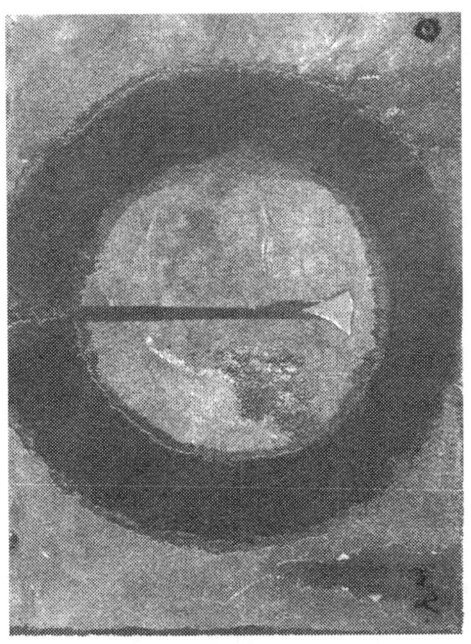

A Romance

by **Eve La Salle Caram**

Plain View Press
P. O.42255
Austin, TX 78704

plainviewpress.net
sbright1@austin.rr.com
1-512-441-2452

ISBN: 1891386-46-8
Library of Congress Number: 2005907969

Cover Art: Anne Monnier, *Message of Love and Peace*, Courtesy of Anne Monnier, Carthothéque romande de al Ville d'Yverdon-les-Bains, and UNICEF.

Books By Eve La Salle Caram:
The Blue Geography
Rena, A Late Journey
Palm Readings, Stories From Southern California (editor)
Wintershine
Dear Corpus Christi

Thanks to Louinn Lota for transcription and proofreading, and to Sharon Kollmeyer for proofreading and special assistance.
For my writing life, thanks as always, toThe Corporation of Yaddo.

For my daughter, Bethel, and her father, Dick, my first encouragers

"This life, which seems so fair,
Is like a bubble blown up in the air
By sporting children's breath
Who chase it everywhere."
William Drummond

"The sky is our absolute nature, which has no barriers
and is boundless, and the ground is our reality,
our relative, ordinary condition."
Sogyal Rinpoche
The Tibetan Book of Living and Dying

"Look at the birds.
Even flying is born
out of nothing. The first sky
is inside you, open
at either end of the day."

Li Young Lee
from *One Heart*

Prologue
Beatrice

I was in the right place all the time, but I couldn't see that until what my grandfather called Wintershine, a glow from the ground frost that sometimes covers quartz and leaves fallen on the path and under bushes, expanded to angelic proportions. (Or to what seemed to me, anyway, the size of large wings.) I was only six, lost I thought in the woods I had trampled through so often, somewhere near the base of North Mountain, tired from the walk and drowsy, almost in a stupor from the cold. If you are in trouble and need help, my grandfather said, sometimes the Wintershine grows and gives it.

A few weeks before I had found in a clearing deep in the woods, rocks which I thought of giving as Christmas presents, quartz and turquoise and some dark ones streaked with gold. On this day I had gone back to claim them and was at an open place, the wrong one I was sure, for I didn't see the treasure. I needed help and the Wintershine grew and gave it.

Years later I reasoned that when light through the pine strikes a half buried crystal — and especially near winter solstice — it creates a giant prism. But back then in the way of children I thought it was an angel. (And in a sense I guess it was.) And that presence ever after hovered over my childhood and threw its beam into my adult years.

So it was my first remembered perceptions of the world had to do with light — slashes of light cutting through the blue-green world that went whirling. I seem to remember watching the world move through these slashes of light from my bassinet under Rob Roy's big oak tree. Rob Roy, whose storybook name had been given to him by his Scottish mother, Anne, who also had one and who died not long after his birth, whitewashed the lower trunks of all our big trees so they would be healthy, live long and well and offer plenty of shade; the wash, he told us, kept blight and bugs away.

Later on, when I was old enough to walk under the trees I saw through slashes of light the leaves on the oak tremble, as well as the violets in the nearby flower beds, their dark leaves and blossoms all trembling. (And then me, too, with all the rest; I saw the shadow of me trembling.)

Our property bordered the hundreds of acres of land that made up the national forest, and at the deepest part of our woods connected to it. Many years later, that connection brought me to the base of the San Gabriels in California. And when childhood's later ties to the Gulf of Mexico broke — and I will soon tell you about our migration into Texas and down its coast to the Gulf — I was delivered to the Pacific and maybe to the whole world (that vast ocean seems most of it.)

But I am getting ahead of myself. It was not on or near water, but in wildwood with an awareness of light that I began. Before I became a global wanderer (at least on the American expanse of it) I only went walking on my grandfather's land and beyond it, just a little into woods that extended to Gulpha Gorge and Iron Springs.

2

I was the only child in a large family of adults, come into the world in a bleak time. Although I was christened Merrill Ann and all of it for my mother's family, (given it I was sure as a bearer of the family sorrow), Merrill being the family's surname and Ann the name of the great grandmother who died young, since I was a small child my Uncle Roy called me "Bea," short for Beatrice in Dante's story, "one" he told me, "who makes others happy." "And one," his wife, my beloved Aunt Ola said, "who is happy, too."

The name stuck. I was from the time I can first remember called "Bea" by almost all my family so that "Bea" was entered above my legal name, even in the family Bible. I was born in the deep heart of the country, southwestern Arkansas near Hot Springs, when it was in the Great Depression. My mother, Louise, was also born there, thirty-four years before delivering me, the only one of her pregnancies she brought to term. I often felt that 1900 was also my real beginning. The year made it easy to keep track of my mother's age.

I write this feeling the need to take you on our journey through the century, the Wintershine my grandfather, Roy, so often spoke of, threaded through even the worst of times. The Depression. The world wars and all the others. But now how do we celebrate, how do we mourn? And what is our liberator?

(Maybe the music that memory makes, the music my mother pursued, that Roy had an ear for, that Robin discovered?)

3

I think not only of Louise, my mother, but of Robby (Robin), her brother, Ola, beloved aunt, Uncle Roy, Ola's husband, the eldest of my grandfather Rob Roy's children (Robby the youngest; another brother, Lloyd came in the middle), and of my grandmother, Nella. Of my father, Edmund, whose roots from his mother's side extend to the northeast, Maine and Massachusetts, I can't say much, for I never knew him or any of his family — the Depression took them. I have pictures and souvenirs from my studies in those places that formed him and mementos in Louise's scrapbooks and cedar chest, and in my head stories, mythology even, but no real memories.

A hole, a big zero — just nothing at all where the memories ought to be.

By the time I could walk from the place where my bassinet once stood to the flower bed with the clumps of violets blowing, and the whole world it seemed to me trembling, they — my father and his people — were gone. In adulthood, in a move to California, I even lost their pictures and for a time regretted having come, in the tradition of my mother's family, so far.

But on our way we also received gifts, crystal rock and seashell, tree bark and pine cone; Texas Gulf to the Atlantic, then a swing all the way over to the Pacific, Ouachita Mountains to the Catskills and Adirondacks during the years when on the trail of his history there I looked for the ghost of my father — but couldn't find it, could not even find his ghost! — and then a stretch over all the land to the San Gabriels, and at last to Diamond Head and Haleakala (where Robby traveled first during World War II) — our American geography, the map of our story, finally joins us to the world. And that liberation, perhaps, is saving.

We are, anyway, experienced travelers, and hardy, having moved completely through the West — the faces and voices of our kin, (Arkansas and Texas), now far back in it — and come out its other side.

Part One

Chapter I
Iron Springs

Beatrice

The first real trip I remember making was with my grandfather who offered it to me as compensation for something I had wanted very much and not gotten, a replacement for my "baby swing," a sturdy contraption in which I was barred in all round. Someone had to stand behind to push me so I would go flying toward the oak leaves and pieces of blue sky.

On the hot summer morning I asked for it, my grandfather refused to make me a new one, not because making such a swing would be difficult or time consuming, (and even then I suspected that it was), but because he thought me too old for it. I was, I believe, going on four, too big to fit into the old, safe swing I loved. When I first asked Roy to build me a swing that morning he quickly agreed, but I saw that what he had in mind as he threw a long white rope over the branch of our oak and brought a piece of newly sawed lumber from the garage as a seat was not what I wanted. I saw no comfort (or even fun, not at first) in the new swing, only challenge, only risk.

"Oh, not that kind, Grandpa," I told him, immediately sorry I had said it for I thought I saw hurt in his face, hurt not to have pleased me, and it always broke my heart a little to see my grandfather, whose dying I finally had to witness, hurt. "Well," he said, "why don't you try this one? You may grow into it, come to like it."

When I refused, he didn't force me into his new skimpy creation. But neither did he take it down. Instead he made another proposition. "You are getting on toward four years old," he told me, "old enough to be a tolerable hiker. Would you like to come with me this morning to Iron Springs?" He pointed to the woods in the back of the house. He said he was going for water and that I could help him carry it, that he needed to fill the canteens. The big one was, he said, all he thought he could carry.

My longing to retreat into the protected territory of babyhood vanished (and in the days that followed, I was a high flyer on the new open swing.)

"You'll be my company and my helper," he said.

And so I began the first of a lifetime of journeys, born as I was into a family that took to them. Barefoot, I ran first thing into the stone side porch of the Little Spanish House as we called the red tiled stucco house my grandfather built to live in after he sold the big white frame on the adjoining property where he had raised his family and quit the contracting business to

raise a few vegetables and some chickens, ran there to get our walking sticks
and the canteens. And to announce to my grandmother that Grandpa had
chosen me to go with him to Iron Springs. My grandmother who I never
remember saying much, made no comment, only handed me the brown
oxfords I hated, which when summer began I had abandoned, scuffed and
worn, by the porch door, left it to me as I sat on the steps, to get in them and
tie the laces. When I finished, Grandpa fastened the khaki ribbons of the
smaller canteen over my left shoulder and thrust the smaller walking stick
into my hand. He took the taller walking stick and slung the already joined
ribbons from the large canteen over his back, pocketed the two apples my
grandmother gave him. "Good bye, Nella," he said, "we'll be back before
supper." And we were off.

Down the back side of the hill where with the Little Spanish House
to one side, Roy and Ola's camp house (built after their good house burnt
down) on it, we were off on a path that passed the big oak under which I
had sat as a baby, the Little Green House built for my mother and me after
my father went away, through a gate and on another path that went past
Grandpa's vegetable garden with greens of all kinds, kale and cabbages and
beautiful new lettuces and green beans on poles set exactly the same number
of inches apart, past this garden of greens (and beets and tomatoes and
onions), around the chicken house where at feed time dozens of baby chicks,
along with the clucking hens, went peeping, and across from the chicken
house, the small cow barn for our milk cow, Bernice, who I tried to milk and
couldn't, but with whom I felt a kinship because I knew her milk had always
fed me and because she had a B in her name ("B" was the letter I learned to
make first); then up what Aunt Ola called "Dread Hill" because she hated to
go up it, through another gate that led into a pine wood — our corn field to
one side of it and a path that led down to a creek and then up another hill
where Old Pete the German man who reeked of the garlic he grew, lived on
the other — the path that we took this day and one that even when I walked
it with my grandfather, I feared.

Old Pete was a foul smelling, rawboned giant of a man who sometimes
bent over me sputtering foreign words and saliva through his coarse red
beard while shaking his huge head of wild red hair. And yet my grandfather,
who had just given him a corner of the property to farm as he pleased (just
because Pete appeared one day and indicated that he wanted it), liked him,
always tipped his hat, patted him on the shoulder and spoke, usually of the
crops or the weather; Pete answered in his own language. Neither understood
what the other said, spoke, it seemed, only for the sake of speaking and
because somehow, in spite of the barrier, they understood each other and had

become friends. Knowing this didn't help. When I saw Pete, the first of many "foreigners" in my life, terror seized me.

And there he was before us, standing in the pathway in front of his gate that we had to go through if we were to turn down the rutted red road that would take us to the Village of Men and then into the deep woods in which we could ascend the path that twisted around the worn mountain that would take us, on its down side, to Gulpha Gorge and Iron Springs.

"Pete," I remember whispering to my grandfather, trembling as I spoke and for the first time since we set out, taking and squeezing his hand. As Pete lumbered toward us, the world fell away from me as it has done many times since.

(The world of my beginning was green or blue green, but as I grew older and moved across a desert or two toward the Pacific, became more blue though green was still in it, and sometimes the brown of pine bark, for as much as I was drawn to oceans — loving and fearing them, — woods also continued to beckon. And through all of this, woods and oceans, slashes of white, and sometimes colored, light. When I was very young — in babyhood — I was always aware of these brilliant slashes, but when I grew older, rarely: only in dramatic flashes now and then. And of course in rainbows, the Scottish ones from my mother's stories about Rob Roy's beginnings, and all the other magical appearances and vanishings, Hawaiian now as I grow old.)

"Pete," I murmured again — or seem to remember murmuring, this long memory being one of my first — my eyes closed, squeezing my grandfather's hand even harder. And then I heard the awful booming guttural sounds, felt the huge rough hand on top of my head. But saw nothing.

"She doesn't meet people much," I heard my grandfather say. "She's scared of people."

"Ja! Ja!" Pete said. Then my grandfather scooped me up in his arms and held me against him, — I still clutched the walking stick in one hand — and I opened my eyes to look over his shoulder past the downside of the hill planted with Pete's garlic.

"Scared," my grandfather said again and laughed. And Pete, also laughing, repeated, "Ja!"

When Grandpa turned and I faced Pete who was smiling, he extended his hand as if to touch me again, but didn't, dropped it to one side, opened his gate for us and waved as we passed him, still sputtering something in his awful tongue.

On the rutted red road that ran past our property and into the deep
woods Grandpa put me down. "Old Pete won't hurt you," he said after we
had walked away. "You mustn't be scared of him. He likes children." I had
been told many times that Old Pete had left all his family when he came
to this country from Germany, had even left his children and that they had
no money to get to him and might never see him again. (I considered them
lucky to have lost such a father and thought I was perhaps not unlucky to
have lost my own.) "Speak to Pete, if you can," Grandpa said, "when you
next see him. You are growing up now, old enough to understand and to not
want to hurt his feelings."

"I'll try," I whispered and walked on. I wanted to tell him that seeing Old
Pete caused me to shake and the whole world to go black and fall away. But I
expect he knew that.

I was about to speak again when I saw the black and white hunting dog
on the other side of the barbed wire that ran along one side of the road and
at the same time saw a couple of fat red squirrels climb up a silver leafed oak
tree. The next thing I knew, the dog was with us on the road and Grandpa
said, "He's away from home. Someone's lost him."

He trotted along beside me at eye level. Then, after we made it around a
long curve in the road, I saw we had come to the Village of Men, so called
because Grandpa said veterans of the Spanish American War (whatever
that was) who wanted nothing more to do with the world, settled there,
helped each other build crude huts out of tree branches and lived in them
without women or children. Or dogs. Grandpa said the friend we had with us
couldn't belong to one of them. Some of the men, silent and unsmiling, sat
on large, flat rocks in front of their houses, and although the sight of them
didn't terrify me the way Old Pete did, I wouldn't have wanted to walk past
them alone.

I looked down at the red road hoping we would soon be by them when
I felt Grandpa touch my shoulder and say, "We turn here." And so we did;
though our black and white friend went straight on. I saw him again and
again on the red road or near it in the wood; he seemed to belong to no
one, to get along without people, and yet he was friendly enough. I thought
of him as the "good dog of the red road." We turned without him and left
that road which had a feeling of safety about it, for a path that cut through
a dark thicket where Grandpa said we had to be careful, to watch carefully
for rattlers since it was summer and they were apt to be out from under
their rocks. When the path narrowed so that there was no room for me to
walk beside my grandfather, he again scooped me up in his arms and held
me against one shoulder. And so we went on, down a steep hill, thick with

trees and briar patches, and on a wider path where Grandpa set me down, up another — hard climbing. So hard that I didn't think I could do it on my own power and began to cry so that Grandpa turned and extended his walking stick. "Take the end of the stick," he said, "hang on." And I did that. Up, up a great hill and then down — held on even though we went down (for the descent seemed to me very steep) through thick trees, mostly pines though I also saw some sweetgum which I had been taught to recognize by their leaves (shaped like stars), thick, thick woods on either side, down, down, down to the bottom of the world, into Gulpha Gorge, a great open pit, where water from what was known as Iron Springs spilled out over the far mountainside.

The gorge darkened as we entered it. As we traveled the black path toward its interior I imagined that the gorge itself, if we ever got there, would be light, had hoped it would be light. Or at least lighter. Grandpa said it was only a little past noon. But it was as if we were entering deepest night. Then the lightning cracked in front of us. Or seemed to, followed by a terrible noise, and Grandpa lifted me to him. "I expect we had better run for it," he said as he struck out, holding me (walking stick, canteen and all) tight against him. His own giant canteen bobbled up and down against his back as he trotted along and the rain struck us, and I watched, somehow comforted by the motion of it, until the awful roar of thunder caused me to close my eyes and I saw no more, but heard my own heart beat, then felt us stop.

We were under an arbor for picnickers. With me still in his arms, Grandpa crouched under one of the cement tables and there we stayed clinging together and trembling. Through cracks in the slats that roofed the shelter, we saw — and sometimes felt — the rain still falling, the lightning popping. We had come all our long way I remember thinking to meet this terror, to be down in this deep, black well. Then just as if my grandfather could read my thoughts, he stroked my cheek and hair, and said, "We'll be all right, darlin'," and I believed him as I believed everything he ever said after.

In weeks and months to come I heard many stories of lightning, the way it had struck the barns and houses and trees of those who lived all around us (though not yet our property) and had killed an acquaintance or two. On our own hill the storm cellar, the other side of the pump, was an honored place, a dozen stone steps leading down to its floor, the walls shelved on every side, the shelves filled with canned fruits and vegetables Ola and my grandmother put up every summer. We fled for it at the first sight of lightning or sound of thunder, and often stayed for hours, finally feasting on beets and carrots and pickled peaches.

But we didn't have it here. Had only a picnic table and each other under our flimsy shelter in this relentless storm. But finally it slackened and Grandpa pulled himself and me with him out from under the table. We saw on the other side of the cavern water falling and through it, colors — chartreuse, and pale blue and mauve and pink and a darker green.

Grandpa pulled himself up from under the table taking me with him and crossed the gorge to the pump by the waterfall with the colored light streaming through it. The water we drew from the pump into our canteens Grandpa said was for healing and for lasting good health for us all. "Honey," he said as he pumped the water and I held the canteens, first one, then the other, under them, "this water is going to be the best thing for your Uncle Roy, get him off that whiskey he is always drinking. I want you to give him your canteen full. The best thing, too, for your Mama; she's always had ailments — hives to female trouble. The iron in this water and the minerals will help all of them. But she needs the water now, too, for her spirit. I'm going to put half of what I draw here in her house." My mother was in some ways Roy's favorite child, though he was also close to Lyman Roy, his eldest and at that time his most tormented son.

I don't remember much about the trip back. The hike home should have been more tiring; we were wet and loaded down — Grandpa's canteen held four quarts, mine two — the ground we went over soggy, but my spirits soared. I knew I had gone a distance not even older children often did, (I doubted that my school age cousin who lived in town had ever gone so far), that I had been selected to help bring back the healing water.

The sun came out before we left the gorge and I remember the walk home as uneventful, hot and long. But I was proud to have made it and from my own canteen to pour a cup of water for my Uncle Roy and later for my mother, proud to have the saving water for those dear to me in my hands.

Chapter Two
Uncle Roy

Uncle Roy said, "This is the best drink, Bea." Why, then did he so often drink from the dark brown bottles that sickened him and us all? That was mysterious, but he had always viewed his life as thwarted, saw some pitch-blackness running through it. None of us knew why he was, in the deepest part of himself, unhappy.

We regarded him as the family genius (and so accepted his pronouncements) and as family seer. Tall and thin, I remember him bent over his work table like a question mark — pale golden freckles on his white hands, fingers stained with the nicotine that probably caused his death — drawing up plans for what he called "a temple" that no one had commissioned him to build. He had taken the plans to most of the ministers in Garland County, not that he had ever visited their churches or would have been welcomed in them.

Although my grandmother was a Methodist and a more or less regular attender, the only churches Lyman Roy ever went near were the Episcopal Church in Hot Springs (because nobody screamed "Hell Fire!" in it, he said, and because it was less architecturally offensive to him than most), and then only at Christmas, when he stood at the back with the latecomers — and the little Negro church on the other side of the fork in Mill Creek Road because he liked the singers. We could hear the men's choir with what Uncle Lyman called "bullfrog singing" all the way to the hill where we lived. "Best bass singing I ever heard," Lyman Roy always said, "Let's take a walk their way." And we set out to draw nearer to the voices, sat on top of a big rock not far from the churchyard to listen. We wouldn't have dreamed of going in, since in those days, in that part of the world, even churches were segregated, black from white. The little frame house where the Morning Star's congregation gathered wanted repair, had holes all through it, in boards, in windows; Uncle Lyman said even its roof leaked. Yet, much as they needed a new building, it would never have entered his head to show his plans for a temple to the minister of this poor black congregation or to any of its members.

But he went on drawing them though none of the white ministers were interested. The Presbyterian minister he went to see who had the funding for a new church, even laughed at his design. And the Baptist minister whose congregation had long since outgrown its one room yellow brick church and wanted something much larger, told Lyman Roy he thought his plans were from the Devil and that he should pray for God's help in keeping decent people out of such a hellish design. "Mr. Merrill," he said, "we all know drink

is your weakness. I believe when you drew these up, you were drinking."
Afterward, Lyman Roy, who had been sober for months, working many
hours a day at his drawing table, visited the liquor store first thing and then
disappeared for a week.

When he returned and sobered up, he took some blueprints out of an old
book and got ready to go back to see the Brother. "It may mean money," he
said to Aunt O. "I can build him what he wants. Any contractor could. He
won't use any building well. I wouldn't want him and his ignoramus followers
in a church of my design."

He said this as he put on the jacket to the suit he always complained
about. He had bought it years back to wear to job interviews. "Wearing this
thing," he told Aunt O, "is worse than having to get in that Army uniform
they locked me into. One day, when I'm overseeing what I want to build,
I won't wear a jacket at all, just comfortable pants and a good white linen
shirt." (Young as I was, I realized then that he was Nella's son and liked fine
fabric, as well as bold but elegant designs.) Then he added, "But if I'm in on
the construction, loose fitting overalls and a work shirt will do fine."

2

After he finished the Baptist job, Uncle Roy went on revising the plans
for his "temple," and when he became discouraged that he would ever find
anyone who was interested in having it built and also had the funds to
put it up, he put the plans aside and took up those he was making for an
underground city and told me wild stories about it. "One day, Bea," he said,
"the world may be so dangerous, so full of poison that people will have to
live underground without air or light."

Much of the time, Uncle Roy literally looked on the dark side, but not
without a macabre humor that often resulted in fanciful surprises, popping
out of a room as he sometimes did in his World War I khakis and gas mask
to give us all a scare. Once in this disguise, he was reluctant to shed it (and
never mind his talk of hating it) and kept his army suit on for days, only
to change into the suit he wore as camouflage, splashes of muted shades of
green all over it, the colors, he said, of the leaves in the Argonne forest.
In this outfit he often patrolled our property, "the hill" as he called it, on
summer holidays, from sun-up on the Fourth of July, and sat around the
house or tramped through the woods in it on winter ones.

I thought of all of his disguises scary and one or two of them funny.
Seeing him in his gas mask was both funny and scary to me. But the scariest

he ever was in a disguise was the Halloween I was four. Aunt O had come back from Kress's with a long gray wig and some granny specks to wear under her witch's hat and with the black robe she had run up herself on the machine. She had made the prettiest costume for me, a full skirted dress with a matching bolero, out of a sweet smelling orange material, shiny as oilcloth and not much thinner, with black cats and witches upon it, the bolero trimmed in black piping. That same piping hung from a ruffled hat of the cats and witches material that she tied under my chin. After Ola finished the hat she took in her head to make her own costume of thin black oilcloth and to get the wig and hat and glasses at Kress's to go with them so that on the night of Halloween we could parade together around the block, one side of which was known as Spencer's Corner, where all the children and grown people walked, very near the center of town in Hot Springs. After dark fell, a street spectacle with bands and twirlers and people in long cars and some on horseback made its way down Central Avenue. "If your Uncle Lyman wants to come," Aunt O said, "I can fix an old sheet up for him and he can follow us and walk behind as a ghost."

"I have something else in mind," Uncle Lyman Roy said when we told him, and he disappeared for a while behind the curtain he and Aunt O drew every night when they went to bed down at the end of the sitting room.

"What are you doing back there, Uncle Roy?" I asked him. But got no answer.

"Pumpkin, let's put your hat on," Aunt O told me. "I expect he's taking a nap and we'll see him later. He doesn't really want to go a-haunting."

Then, just as I turned to go, Uncle Lyman Roy jumped out from behind the curtain, but at first I didn't know it was him. I though a real witch had come to get us and I screamed, for that is what I saw before me — a witch in funny glasses and a pointed hat over long, gray hair and Aunt O's chenille bedspread wrapped around her. But then I saw Uncle Roy's old army boots on her feet and his camouflage suit through a gap in the meeting place of the two sides of the spread he tried to hold together.

"Lyman!" Aunt O screamed. "I'll swear. You'll scare the life out of us! Now give me my clothes." And he popped his wig and hat off laughing and put it on her head and she laughed too, and told us he would drive us to Spencer's corner where everyone paraded and past which the mayor would ride on a white horse, and where in the Corner Café we could get hot chocolate after we had walked around. When we got home, we could roast marshmallows in our wood stove, Betsy's fire.

And we did all that and, after, Uncle Lyman Roy read to us, a scary story or two from the dime store book he had about witches and ghosts and some were funny and made us laugh. And then when I asked, he read from "the other" book, the one he liked best and often read from. The cover was so worn that no one could see it's title, but Uncle Roy always said, "These are old Greek stories," and he read about Perseus who cut off the head of the woman with snakes for hair and about Demeter and her daughter, Persephone, who was against her will, taken down to the underworld — had been abducted by its king — when the dark like what we had at Halloween came, and then he read a happier story about a flying horse named Pegasus who charged off into a sky filled with light.

That was the story I liked best. I didn't learn to ride as a child — by the time I was born, the days of traveling by horseback were gone. But I had heard how my mother had ridden horses everywhere when she was growing up and when Grandpa and Grandma were young there was no other way with any speed to get around. It was hard for me to imagine my indoor grandmother on horseback, but my mother told me that Grandma had done her share of riding and that my grandmother and grandfather went for Sunday afternoon rides, just for pleasure, when Louise was a little girl. Later, they got a car and then another, which the family still had, a Studebaker we called The Old Bus, which we took maybe twice a month on shopping trips to town. Grandpa never learned to drive, and rather than try to learn on The Old Bus, walked to town when I was a child. He prided himself on being able to walk far, and of bringing up several children, Lyman Roy and my mother, and of at least one grandchild (me) who were as he said, "great walkers," too.

But although I had not ridden a horse, and mostly saw people on horseback in parades, I day-dreamed of the days when people rode and over and over asked for the story of Old Peg as Uncle Lyman Roy called the storybook horse who with a tap of his hoof brought a fountain out of the mountain — had he maybe a long time ago done that in the gorge and brought forth Iron Springs? — and who, besides that, had wings!

"Bea," Uncle Lyman Roy said, "we'll teach you to ride and one day you should have a fine horse." I didn't get one, though I did learn to ride a little when I was older, but I liked to hear and tell stories of horses and I drew many pictures of horses, or tried to. I never did capture the likeness of the Pegasus I imagined. No matter how you try to do it, a horse with wings is hard to catch.

As I have said, the Methodists and Presbyterians, and even most of the Baptists, Uncle Lyman Roy found out, either had churches that suited them fine or no money to build churches that would suit them better. Lyman Roy never thought to show the plan for his church to Reverend Peabody, the minister at The Church of the Morning Star. But one day, when Reverend Peabody came across him on the road, at the place where it forks — both Lyman Roy and the Reverend were on their way to town — the Reverend asked. This was just a few days after Uncle Lyman had spoken to Reverend Peabody outside his church.

We woke up that Sunday morning, as we often did, to the sound of the bass singing that reached us on our hill on our part of the Mill Creek Road from the hollow on the other side of it and several green hills where The Church of the Morning Star sat, a plain little white frame structure shamefully in need of repair, in spite of its beautiful name. After we put our clothes on and had our coffee (mine was half milk and sugar in one of Aunt O's pretty demitasse cups), Lyman Roy said, "Bea, let's you and me set out on a walk, see how close we can get to those bullfrog singers." Then he imitated their sound – "doe, doe, doe, doe" — his voice getting deeper with every note.

I always loved the trips we took to the singing: we walked quickly so we could get to the heart of it faster, even skipped for part of the way, though we knew we weren't in danger of missing it. The Morning Star's services were mostly singing (mostly male bass) and went on, sometimes, for half the day. I knew after we arrived we would sit on the big, flat rock outside for some time. (I liked to lie on my back there and through oak leaves look up at patches of sky.) On this day, however, the service seemed shorter than usual — we only got through one or two hymns, and after they were over, Reverend Peabody and his congregation came out to greet us first thing. "Mr. Merrill," he said (everyone in the country knew Lyman Roy because of all the bridges he and my grandfather had built, and half of Reverend Peabody's congregation had been in on some of the labor.) "I look out my window some Sundays and I see you and the little girl and I want you to know we would be pleased for you to come in for a service." Reverend Peabody was a young man who acted like an older one and who spoke differently from any man, black or white, I had ever heard. He was, Uncle Roy said, new to the country, come from Illinois. That's why he called Lyman Roy "Mr. Merrill." Any other black man, minister or not, would have called him "Mr. Roy," identifying him with my grandfather whom they knew as "Mr. Rob." Uncle

Lyman just nodded and smiled in that wry way he had. "Much obliged," he said — but even as he spoke I knew we would never go inside the church — and then he added, "Your choir is good."

A few days later, when the Reverend saw Lyman Roy on the road, he said (or so Lyman Roy told me), "Mr. Merrill, the last time I saw him, your father told me you were working on plans for a church. We have no funds for a building, though we surely could use one. But I'd like to look at your plans all the same." Reverend Peabody came by the little pineboard house that very afternoon and looked at the plans and talked to Lyman Roy about them. "You see," Uncle Lyman said, "it's a simple design and except for the skylights, the cost will be minimal."

"I've never seen anything like this," Reverend Peabody said, but not in a disparaging way.

Later Aunt O told me Reverend Peabody was the only person who had ever seen the plans who didn't think they were crazy. "Most people think it's real strange that your uncle wants to build a round church with a ceiling full of skylights. They say it's a crazy idea in a country of lightning storms, but your Uncle Lyman believes if his church ever does go up, the lightning itself will admire the building too much to strike. Of course he told me that," she added, "when he was guzzlin' hooch."

"I heard Reverend Peabody say it surely would be a place to praise the Lord and even with all the glass in the ceiling he knew the Almighty would keep those inside safe. He was just sorry his congregation could never afford to have it."

"Bea," Uncle Roy said after Reverend Peabody had shook his hand and gone down our path, "if I win enough at the track I'll give that black Yankee Reverend the money to do the job. He has sense and a bunch of good singers. Never mind what these ignoramuses around here say about his color. It's come to me that he and his congregation deserve my church."

4

A day or two after Reverend Peabody's visit, Uncle Lyman Roy took me to the races with him. Aunt O said that when he was drinking, he ran to the races all the time, a dangerous practice, she said, for he never won.

"Pumpkin," she told me, "I used to go with him, but we never won anything and I vowed to quit."

Sometimes when he disappeared — and he would, and would be gone for days and days with the whole family, or at least the women, praying over him in their various ways. "Take the Devil out of him!" my grandmother whispered over her wood cook stove as she stirred cornbread in a skillet for a Sunday supper she knew her eldest child would not be home to eat, while Ola, looking out the windows on the dining porch as she set the table, said right out loud to the twilight, "Let him know we love him and bring him home."

After a while, a whole week sometimes, Roy would come staggering up the hill with a small sack of groceries and empty pockets and afterwards, he'd sleep for days, only rising to cook and eat and drink Iron Springs water, saying every time he took a cup full of it, "This is the best drink, Bea. You stick to this."

And then one morning he would rise and go to his drawing board and work long hours there day after day and sometimes month after month, half of the time drawing up more plans for his "temple" that nobody, except possibly, Reverend Peabody who had no money, wanted him to build, until he disappeared again.

But on this day, when he took me to the races, he was sober and only drank black coffee and bought me peanuts and Dr. Pepper and pointing to the racing form, asked, "What name do you like? 'Sonny's Delight?' 'Peg O My Heart?' 'Pretty Places?'"

And of course I said, "The one named Peg." And he bet a few dollars, but lost those.

"Bea, we lost," he said. "But we won't always lose. We'll come again."

And afterwards, he showed me the horses in their stalls and introduced me to one of the jockeys. "Did you know your granddaddy wanted to be a jockey?" he asked, and I shook my head. "Well, he did. He was a small man you know, and wiry, and when he was younger he sure could ride! One day, Bea, we'll get you a horse and I'll teach you."

By the time I was old enough to learn and my Uncle Lyman Roy had enough money to buy the horse — the year I turned thirteen — he had cancer of the throat, diseased some said from all the liquor that had gone down it, and was gone. But all thorough my childhood, I dreamed some of riding a horse like Peg O My Heart, a light colored filly who hadn't won the race, (so we couldn't take home any money), but who had come in third, and I loved the stories my mother told about her riding when she was a hot-headed girl.

Chapter Three
Louise

She would tell me as we sat in moonlight on the screened in sleeping porch of The Little Green House summer nights when it was too hot to sleep, tell me as she sipped from a tin cup of water from Iron Springs, her dark hair and green eyes shining. Oh, I thought she was very pretty. And her voice was low and warm and the stories she told, like the sweet syrup my Aunt O made from the berries she picked in the deep woods thicket, flowed on and on.

Stories about Grandmother Melrose's farm and the horses she rode there. The paradox was this: my mother, wild and vibrant as she had been, and was to continue being much of the time through the century, was always recovering from some illness, bronchitis and maybe a touch of TB, and nervous collapse in her teens, then malaria in her twenties (Uncle Lyman Roy said she wouldn't live through the decade), in her thirties, miscarriages, then a childbirth that nearly killed her followed by piles so bad that doctors finally took a third of her intestine out. In her forties she suffered a fibroid tumor the size of a newborn; in her fifties, pneumonia and again in her sixties, cancer at seventy, stroke at ninety and after that, a broken hip and what she called "sinking spells," which caused her to all but lose consciousness, bruised skin and bones. But through all this she maintained a tough resilience, and a palpable life.

"I always loved to ride!" she told me, and then went on about it for some time.

She said: "Maybe I got my love for horses from your granddaddy who wanted to be a jockey, or even from your Uncle Roy who didn't ride much but who was always at the track!

"I can't remember a time when I didn't ride. I think I was on horseback when I was as small as two or three.

"Was that a good thing? I don't know. Seems to me sometimes that people who acquire things stay in one place — while members of this family let everything they own go and strike out all over the country and always have, following some excitement, some promise, but mostly just because it is in us — oh a wild, gypsy streak! — to go.

"Has that kept us from having anything?

"Sure we go farther — your Uncle Roy gallivants all over looking for jobs, and Daddy went once as far as New Mexico, and that was partly for me, for my sickness, (I had spots on my lungs) and God only knows where the war will take Robby, but do we get ahead?

"The earliest trips I remember were all pleasant. We took the riverboat, the Stacker Lee, to Grandma's in the summer. Boarded at Memphis, and the next day Aunt Myria's husband, Dr. Artrum, met us. Aunt Myria was one of your grandmother's big sisters, your grandmother the youngest in a family of twelve, ten girls and two boys, Willie and Blaze being the oldest. Willie, who spent most of his time in the fields, didn't speak much, but Blaze, who was bossy, made up for him. Always giving orders. I liked to help with the planting, but hated the way Blaze spoke to me. 'Move along now, Missy. And watch what you do.' In my mind, Dr. Artrum, city-bred in Chicago, was the only real man in the family, or anyway, the only one I cared about.

"Dr. Artrum wore goggles and a big, funny looking hat and a duster when he drove his car to the Illinois farm where Grandmother Melrose lived, maybe twenty-five miles away from the place where the boat docked. I loved to speed along in that roadster with him!

"Oh I was excited just to see him waiting to meet us when we got off the riverboat, in his driving outfit and his shiny car. And what a thrill to ride in it, bumping along those dirt roads, dust a flying, the green fields stretched out on either side.

"Those summers — the beginning of them anyway — when I was a little girl were all thrill. We took the train to Memphis where we boarded the Stacker Lee, so excited we stayed awake almost all night, telling stories and singing songs and eating sandwiches and cake from the basket your grandmother brought along, counting the hours until the boat docked in St. Louis the next day. And before we knew it, as I've said, Dr. Artrum waited to take us to Grandmother Melrose's farm in Ellery, Illinois. We would stay you know all of June and July and into August — your grandmother and me and Robby who was just a baby — leaving our menfolk back in Arkansas, your grandfather and Roy, who was a grown man by this time, and Lloyd, who was just a teen-ager, seventeen, but who had already married and started his own business.

"Summers seemed to go on forever, and oh, I wanted them to. I didn't stay in the house much — that was for your grandmother and her mother, my grandmother, and most of the women (though some of my aunts did work in the fields sometimes) and Robby who was just a toddler as I've told you. I didn't know what they did and didn't care; whatever it was, it was dull, I reckoned. I liked to be out in the fields with the men. My grandfather had been killed in the Civil War, leaving my grandmother with eleven children and a three-hundred-and-twenty-acre farm! I didn't appreciate what a responsibility that was. I thought it was all fun, and just for fun, I'd help plant and plough. 'Keep the eyes up when you drop the potatoes in,' I remember Uncle Blaze always ordered. And though I didn't like the way he spoke to me, I loved that, dropping the tiny potatoes in rows, seeing that all the eyes were up! I guessed they couldn't grow unless their eyes were up to catch, through the dirt, at least a ray or two of the sun.

"I liked to plant and I liked to ride even if your great grandmother Melrose did assign me to the slowest horse on the farm. I rode all over the place all summer and on the hottest days. From horseback I could see what was really going on.

"One day, I got a glimpse from the path through the field of Dr. Artrum over on the road in his fancy driving clothes and flashy car and I dug my heels into Mary Lou — the old pokey horse my grandmother had given to me to ride — so I could catch up to him. 'Why whoa there, Petty,' (he always called me that, I don't know why, slang for 'Pretty,' I guess) when he saw me turn out of the property and gallop toward him, 'do you want to break your neck?'

"'I'll race you,' I yelled. Even on Mary Lou, who I had to kick in the side over and over to get going, I thought I might beat him to the driveway of Grandma's house.

"And do you know I did? I expect maybe he slowed down some to let me. But maybe not. God knows I could make a horse trot.

"Years later when I was in music school in Chicago, Dr. Artrum who by that time was gray-headed but who still cut a figure in fine clothes, came to the Three Arts Club where I was living to take me out to dinner at the Palmer House, and I was so excited. But it turned out to be a sad evening, for we hadn't been seated at the pretty table in the dining room long when he said, 'Petty, Nella asked me to tell you that your Grandmother Melrose is dead and that Blaze has the farm up for sale.' By this time your grandmother's sisters had all married and Uncle Willie was also dead and gone.

"After that, memories of summers in Illinois were all I had, but I treasured them, and still do."

2

While my mother spoke, I often colored in one of my books. My favorite was the big Mother Goose I'd had so long I thought maybe I had been born with it and whose verses I knew by heart, loving their sounds, not caring what any of them meant or didn't mean. The book was large, well bound and handsome with tough, shiny pages, illustrations in bright colors on every one. It must have been expensive, a sacrifice for someone — whoever had bought it for me, (and I didn't know who) in those hard times. But I was never reprimanded for coloring, or making my letters, in it. I could make words with them long before I entered school. I colored all the figures that were sketched in black and white and added some of my own. With a silver crayon — I still remember the luster of it — I tried to capture something of Louise as she spoke, the movement of her hand, the shine on her hair.

She said, "Those summers were an idyll. I don't remember quarreling with my mother, your grandmother, when I was very young. Maybe I just didn't see enough of her to do it, for I not only rode in the summertime. I rode at home, too.

"Rode Bob, the wild stallion that your granddaddy said nobody else could mount, let alone go anywhere. Everyone said he was mean, but I knew better; he was just strong willed — so he and I understood one another — a strong spirited animal who had to be free. But he let me on him and he never threw me once. I was light on him, I guess, but he knew that, otherwise, I was his match, that we were two of a kind. Rode him bareback all over the mountainside and down our road, just hunkered way down on him and squeezed and directed him with my hands in his mane, and on his sides as much as I could — I was no more than nine or ten — with my legs and thighs. We galloped down Mill Creek Road and into town and up Hot Springs Mountain and when the cousins saw me (your grandmother's niece's children), they shrieked and cried and called your grandmother on the telephone to say they had seen me and that people were talking about the family that would let a little child, and a girl at that, ride a wild horse bareback and sometimes shoeless; that it wasn't proper, and that, besides, they were sure I was going to be killed. (I expect one or two of them even hoped I might be.) And your grandmother would tell your grandfather to stop me next time — 'The whole countryside is talking,' she said — but he never paid any attention, (and she seldom went out of the house.)

"In the winter it was harder to get out. Sometimes it rained for weeks or just misted and frosted with cold. I practiced piano all through the time I wasn't in school — three and four hours after I got home sometimes and I lost myself and all my troubles in the music, freed by my practice and the scores created by — who knew what or who?

"Mozart, Schumann, Brahms, were the names on the music. But I wondered about it — where it really came from.

"The music, going deep into it, losing myself, was what I wanted. But sooner or later, your grandmother pulled me away.

"One winter night I'll always remember. I had not long before turned thirteen.

"I was deep in, being pulled away when she called me.

"'Louise, come in this kitchen and help me peel potatoes.' Potatoes like the ones I'd put in the ground for Uncle Willie, I expected, all their eyes up. But I didn't care about them this time.

"To hell with all the chores. I banged the lid down on the piano, walked into the kitchen to the pile of potatoes and paring knife waiting for me on the counter, looked over at Nella — in the corner of the dining porch, stooped over the supper table, a mean expression on her face (there was always a mean expression it seemed to me) — picked up the paring knife, then hurled it at her. But it missed, (I guessed I knew it would) went sailing by her into a corner crack in the rock wall. She didn't even flinch — that's the way she was when fury rose in her, stone still, but I knew she would call to Daddy for the razor strap.

"Lloyd came in then and said, 'Hello, Maw, hello, Sis. Do you know Old Tom just came in?' (Old Tom, you know was the cat who had come out of the woods to live with us and sometimes slept with the chickens.)

"I ran past Lloyd. Damn him anyway. Damn Old Tom. Damn my mother and her potatoes. Damn all of them, this whole family. Not one of them could think of anything but household matters. And I, inside the music had been with Beethoven, at least for a little while, had been near the heart of — what?

"What I could only think of as 'the hum.' The hum of, oh I don't know how to say this. But of everything — wonderful and terrible — everything I was and everything in the world.

"That's crazy I guess and maybe I was crazy, too. ('Crazy Louise,' that's what your grandmother's nieces always called me and on this day I heard my mother scream it at me, too.)

"Anyway, I ran past her screaming, past Lloyd, ran down the steps past Old Tom, the wild woods cat we had adopted or who had adopted us and out toward the barn and Bob.

"Never mind the cold and mist. Never mind that the short coat I wore was an old, worn out jacket I pulled from a peg on the wall. I would mount and ride him down the hill, down the road and on into the mountain. They said he was a wild horse and that I was a wild girl to ride him. Well damn them! Damn them! We'd be wild together. Hellzapoppin was what I sometimes called him. That night Bob became his second name. Hell was popping all right, in him and in me."

Chapter Four
Louise

"And we rode and rode. Down Mill Creek and into town and up Hot Springs Mountain and down and out the other side of town, and out of Garland County.

"Until finally we were on the acreage your grandfather and Roy had bought in Pike County, oh, maybe fifteen miles away, the rockiest in the state, where when I was a very little girl, your granddaddy would take me. We cut bags full of holly off the big bushes, more like trees really, to decorate the house for Christmas. And we also found, sometimes, hanging from the oaks, lots of mistletoe.

"I remember often going when it was foggy.

"And it sure was this night on old Hellzapoppin Bob.

"Your grandfather never told me, as he told you and I guess some others about the Wintershine. But he said it was good to get the berries on a real dim day because the red and green of them, the shine on the green leaf, would make it bright. I don't remember going holly picking in any other kind of weather. During these times your granddaddy spoke of the reason for wanting these flat fields full of big holly bushes and white oak trees. 'I'd like to move out this way one day,' he said, 'it's real country.' Where we lived he said was still too close to town. 'Didn't used to be,' he said, 'not when your mother and I first got the place, but the town's pushed out since then. In Pike County, town's still a long way away. We could fish in the creek from Caddo River, which cuts through, and swim in the ponds that are right here on the property.'

"He went on sometimes for the better part of the morning, talking about his dream. He planned to build bird baths with the rocks he could pick up in the county, quartz and colored pyrites — oh there were so many different kinds — and use them also to line a goldfish pond.

"He made living out on the acreage in Pike County sound like going to Heaven. 'Well' I remember telling him as we walked into an acre of cedars, 'at Christmastime we would never want for holly or mistletoe, or a tree.'

"And as we walked, your granddaddy dreamed aloud and on and on. 'Here's where we would put our house,' he said as we came to a clearing near the back of the property, the crest of a little hill that swooped down to a little bit of water, a creek that was just a trickle off the Caddo, but which Daddy said got fuller further on. 'We'd be hidden away,' your grandfather said. 'Nobody but God would ever find us back here.'

"Then in his talking he constructed the house, and gave it a broad front porch which faced the front of the slope with the creek down below, its big parlor and dining room and the room just for my music and my piano where I could shut the door and lock it if I liked and play and play all day. 'You could keep the key in your pocket if you liked,' he told me. 'Nella would never be able to get in.' And he'd chuckle, but then tell me that he would give her a room to sew in, in the back of the house across the hall from the kitchen and she could keep the key to that. Upstairs he said he'd have a room to read in when he got tired of reading on the porch, 'a room just for reading,' he said. The whole family could use it if they had a mind to. (Except for Roy I didn't think anybody much would. You would have, but this was years before you came along.) And in it he'd keep his newspapers and books, and he'd also have a bedroom for each of his children so each would have a private place at home.

"As I sat on that slope, Bob tied to a slender tree, I saw the house to one side of me rising, then walked toward it, and in my mind climbed its steps, played Beethoven in my piano room, sat in the fine parlor, then slept, took a nap, in the room just for me on the second floor.

"Your granddaddy had all but talked his dream, which was the best I ever heard, into coming true. And on that dark, cold evening, after my wild ride in fury down a country road and up and down a mountain and down a main street to another country road and out and across two counties into the holly fields that belonged to us where I dismounted and tied wild Bob to a tree, I felt a calm come over me, saw and entered Daddy's dream house there. And it gave me rest.

"And he talked about it all through my childhood. But sometimes he'd talk about his mother, too — Annie, who had come to America from Scotland, who had given him the name of a countryman from a storybook and then died. Died all that long time ago. He couldn't remember how old he was, but he didn't think he'd been born and in the world too long. He could barely remember his mother, but often he said he felt her near, and particularly near Christmastime, especially he once told me on days when it was foggy or just misty and dark. He didn't know why. Annie Laurie McIvor, named by her father and mother after the girl in the song, had left Scotland in childhood, but had been born in a craggy place near Edinburgh. Maybe, he said, only the weather she had been born in could bring her forth in this new country.

"Anyway, it was on a dark evening with just a little frosty shine on it. I had ridden Bob down our hill and onto Mill Creek Road and into town and up and down Hot Springs Mountain and down the main street, Central

Avenue which had cars on it even then and out the highway through all
of Garland and into Pike County and into the very fields where my Daddy
had taken me as a child. We had sixty acres and all of the flat front of the
property was covered with holly and evergreens and big oak trees, some
dangling mistletoe and I rode into them on and on, but stopped, halted
young Bob fast when I saw a shape, then shapes before me. I couldn't see
what the biggest and most mysterious was, could only make out a swirling
mass the other side of the cedar forest, just near the spot in the clearing
where our house would have stood. I didn't know what it was, didn't see her
in it, our Annie Laurie. But the small shapes in front of me became distinct
the moment I stopped Bob and slid off him.

"Little people with round faces and curly, golden hair, the largest just
a tiny lady in a bright pink dress that shimmered with silver buttons. The
others were no bigger than dragonflies, but each distinct, and all of them
dancing. Happy things. All with beautiful round smiling faces. All girls.

"And I saw them clearly. They weren't like the larger shape that had
frightened me at first — they weren't ghosts. I watched them mesmerized. I
wasn't afraid. I wanted to speak but couldn't. Paralysis set in. But finally I did
reach out. I wanted to touch them. But they vanished when I tried and Bob
and I were alone.

"I mounted Bob then, both of us calm and rode through the cedar trees,
then stopped and slid off Bob on the other side — the big shape I had seen
that frightened me gone (I'm sure now a connection to Daddy's mother!)
— where I broke some holly from the branches of two or three of the holly
bushes to take back to the house. An offering for Nella who I suddenly had a
rush of tender feeling for, and I had surely hated her an hour or so before.

2

"They say, you know, that something is wrong with me — with my
head — that dreams from the nighttime and daytime, too, appear before
me as if they are real. And that I had better watch out. Well, I don't know,
but I don't think I see dreams, baby. I'm not like your father. Or even
your grandfather. I've never been a dreamer. Life is what I'm after. Drama.
Action! (Like in the music I play and then hear repeat and repeat over and
over in my head.) What comes before me is real!

"That golden-haired one, realer than real.

"After the day I first saw her, I took Bob to the holly fields often. It was the best place to be alone. To walk. And to see ahead. To see my way through.

"Nella had put that first holly I brought her in a blue vase that had belonged to her mother — my grandmother Melrose — which she brought to Arkansas when she first came from Illinois. She liked the holly from those wild bushes, prickly stuff that it was, which seemed odd to me, for I thought of Nella as liking very little, and nothing at all that wasn't smooth or tame.

"She had a taste for egg custard, vanilla icing and, yes, velvet and velveteen (but kept the velveteen sofa shrouded except for Christmas Day.)

"She truly loved materials, skimped on groceries to buy good ones. And I looked forward to the new dresses I knew she would make for me at the beginning of each season. Uncle Blaze always said your grandmother was spoiled, that it was because she was the baby of the family that she never had to work in the fields like most of her sisters, and because she was good with a needle. She made all the clothes for the family by the time she was thirteen.

"Oh she could copy anything. Hubert Mendleson gave her permission to copy designer originals so she could make them for all the Methodist ladies in Hot Springs. He said Nella Merrill's copies were good publicity for Mendleson's store. Once your grandmother had made their dresses, the ladies would go into Mendleson's for other things, petticoats and corsets, stocking and handbags and ribbons for their hair and once in a while for a broach or necklace or some other expensive thing. Your grandmother was a genius with a needle. She never needed a pattern. She loved clothes, lived to make them. Worked so hard most of her life that she didn't have too much of a chance to wear her best ones. But she did on holidays. And on Sundays. I always said she went to church so she could dress up.

"Well, out there in the holly fields I thought some about your grandmother. Most of the time, she and I were crossways, just didn't get along.

"She didn't like me, always seemed to prefer her boys. 'I had three boys,' she always said, 'and Louise gave me more trouble than any of them.'

"But she said she didn't want any of her children, that all of them were accidents. Robby, of course, who came along late in her life, was the biggest surprise. She said she hadn't planned for him, but would make him a pleasure. And he became a Mama's boy, always by her side, at the sink and sewing machine — drying her dishes, threading her needles. Daddy told her she was ruining him, but he never could get her to turn him loose outside. Once in a while, when he did go, the other boys would taunt him, call him

Chapter Five
Louise

"I didn't know how marriage and childbirth and the Depression would stop me. When I rode out to the holly fields and lay on my back on the slope where our house would be or ran down it to wade in the creek and skip some rocks across it, I was hell-bent on having the life intended for me, the life I clearly saw.

"And it seemed if I could just be by myself without interference from other people I could have it. By myself so I could concentrate and so I could practice. That was why when the whole family went off on outings I always begged to stay home. All of them, it seemed to me, were forever going somewhere. God knows this family is a band of gypsies and just strikes out for destinations all over the United States.

"But I was never big on travel, except as you know on horseback, though I've done my share of it, and as a child someone was always jerking me off to go somewhere. 'Please,' I always asked when your grandmother proposed that we go gadding — to town to shop or to the county fair or to spend some time with my cousins who lived in Hot Springs or Malvern, 'please, could I stay home?' And when I was old enough, eight or nine I guess, she let me.

"And when they were all gone, all the family, I would play the piano and sing. I could be as loud as I liked with everybody gone so that later the neighbors — who lived way up the road — would ask your grandmother who we had staying with us that sang. After I had finished, I stood up by the side of the piano bench to take a bow and I heard the audience applauding and some in it even sending up a cheer!

"Oh, I practiced my scales and spent hours playing the great music — as best I could do it then — too.

"That was the only time I ever really enjoyed home, that is in the house, when I was growing up. Nella woke me every morning before the light with the boom-boom-boom of her broom handle on the kitchen ceiling under my bedroom floor, my signal to get up and practice scales. The piano had cost too much, I heard her tell Daddy, for me not to do it. And I never minded practicing anything. But I hated having to get up in cold and dark and half-asleep. Oh, it was doing her bidding all those dreary mornings that helped break me. I had a breakdown, you know, when I was sixteen and developed an infection in my lungs — they thought for a while I had TB, — so that Daddy had to move the whole family to New Mexico, worked as a hand on the Matador Ranch near Clayton, and your Uncle Roy, too — Daddy finally convinced the whole family to come along — because Uncle Doc said the air there would cure me.

"If your grandmother didn't have me practicing in the dark, she had me polishing furniture, or peeling vegetables and snapping beans. In the late afternoon hours, when I wanted to be at the piano, she called me away from it. The only peace I had was when she and all the others went gallivanting, or when I rode Bob out to the holly fields which for a long time I thought of as just mine and Daddy's.

"And when we left for New Mexico, it was only those fields — those fields and Bob — I missed."

2

"New Mexico healed me, at least as much as I was going to be (I had spots on both my lungs from the bronchitis I had always been prone to, and a nervous breakdown and to this day I can't take loud noises or even to hear someone slurping coffee or crunching celery or rattling a popcorn sack.) Your grandmother let me sleep there because Uncle Doc had said I needed rest. The New Mexico doctor said I should sleep on an open porch and I still remember waking under pounds of blankets with snow blowing across the bed.

"I left high school before my senior year was out just before we went (the infection in my lungs was so serious), but finished by correspondence and got my diploma. And being out of school, I never had to get up early, I never did again in my life if I didn't have to. The main house had a piano and Mrs. Lucas, who owned the ranch, let me play it later in the day.

"And after two winters and a summer, we made our way back to Arkansas. Your grandfather hadn't sold the house, only put some of your grandmother's good for nothing relation in it. And they were pretty ornery because when we got back most everything needed work. But they did feed the animals and milk Bernice.

"One of them even tried to saddle and ride Bob, though we had warned them all not to, and Bob put the one that did it in the hospital with broken ribs. (He said after that it was hard to get much done on the place. Just like one of your grandmother's relations to use my Bob as an excuse.) And after that, your grandmother decided we had to get rid of Bob and that made me want to kill her. It just broke my heart.

"'That horse is crazy,' I heard her tell your granddaddy. 'We have to get rid of him. Find somebody to sell him to.'

"Daddy told her it wouldn't be easy to find a buyer for a horse that most of the time didn't want a rider.

"'Well then,' I heard Mama say, 'just take him off.'

"'Take him where, Nella?' Daddy asked.

"'I don't know — way up, up the country somewhere. Some of those ignorant hill people might take him, might think he could be trained. Or take him down to Blanche's sister in Louisiana — she always wanted another horse.'

"I couldn't stand to hear anymore and ran to Bob right away, flew to the holly fields, (and said I never would return), Bob in a high gallop all the way.

"And when we got there and I slid off of Bob and tied him to the white oak at the top of the hill next to the spot where Daddy and I were going to put our house, I threw myself on the ground and sobbed and sobbed — until I was exhausted and fell asleep.

"But then a hand on my shoulder brought me awake and when I stirred I saw your granddaddy next to me; he had ridden the old gray he loved so much to find me — you know he never did learn to drive a car. 'Honey,' he said, 'I know how you feel, but there's no arguing with your mother when her mind is set. I'll have to send him away.'

"'Daddy,' I said, 'I've been riding him since I was little. Stand up to her. Tell her Bob is my horse. That if she sends him off, she'll be sending off part of me. Talk to her, Daddy.'

"A cooling wind from the Caddo blew over us as he held me close. And he said, 'I will.'

"But there was no dissuading your grandmother. After I came home and went to bed, I heard them quarreling well into the night. And Bob was gone by morning. I went to look for Bob in his stall in the barn at break of day. He was gone and your grandmother, I soon learned, was gone with him. When your granddaddy was asleep she had called Blanche — Old Hatchet Face, your Uncle Lyman called her — and asked her to bring her good for nothing son and no account husband — Uncle Lyman Roy said he was no account even if he was the county judge — and their horse trailer with her. And the four of them got Bob and went away. Your grandmother left a letter for your granddaddy which he found when he came in from feeding the chickens and milking. In it she said she was going to Louisiana for a while to stay with Blanche's sister, Nelsie. When I came in the house from Bob's empty stall, your grandfather gave it to me. 'I'm sorry, honey,' he said. 'Your mother's gone for awhile and Bob with her.'

"I never wanted to see my mother again. And I knew my time had come, that it was my time to go traveling whether I liked it or not.

"Oh, I fought taking off and argued with myself and all the forces that be. 'I don't want to go to some other new place,' I said to just about anybody who asked me. 'I don't want to spend my life just tramping around.'

"But I had to admit that I could no longer live in the same house with my mother — after she came back we barely spoke to one another — and opportunity seemed elsewhere. Besides, I could see everything was changing. In the summer of 1917, Lyman Roy left us, shipped off for France and the war.

"By October, my bags were packed for Chicago where I had an audition for a job playing the organ at the Palace Theatre. I knew if I got on as an organist I could pay board at the Three Arts Club where I already had a reservation and for lessons with one of the finest teachers.

"'Never tell anybody you're from Arkansas,' was the first piece of advice my teacher gave me.

"And I never did — oh, to think how Daddy loved all the Arkansas country, but especially the Ouachitas that he was so homesick for all the time he was in New Mexico. So homesick that he had to come back to them, even though Mrs. Lucas wanted him to stay and was kind and good to all of us.

"Although Daddy was homesick, your Uncle Robby really flourished on the Matador Ranch, which was owned by the Lucas family who had come all the way from Scotland to buy it in 1907, the year he, Robby, our Robin, was born.

"Mrs. Lucas let him play in her attic and all her closets, dress up in her old high-heeled shoes and jewelry — he wore some of it in a featured role she cast him in, a shepherd boy who speaks to an angel, in the ranch's Christmas play. She draped him for the part in one of her old flimsy evening dresses and the angel gave him a rhinestone tiara Mrs. Lucas had worn as a girl in Edinburgh, as a sign. But he got on with some of the ranch hands, too — not all and one really had it in for him — learned Spanish from them, and even learned to sit on a horse and looked so good on it that Mrs. Lucas gave him his very own pony.

"He loved the ranch even though one of the hands picked on him and a bad thing happened during the first winter of our stay. He broke both of his arms in the elbows for a second time when he slid off the roof of the main house — we thought trying to fly.

"(The first time he broke his arms because he fell off the roof of the Arkansas house which he had climbed onto from a tree. After they were broken twice — and both times from a tumble from a rooftop, he could never lift anything much. That's why he was never sent into active duty in the war.) The angel in the play — and would you believe she was your Aunt Ola? — had flown off the stage or seemed to. (Mrs. Lucas had her pulled up on wires.) Maybe he thought he could find her. Ola always said that Robby early on tried to make his way to God. And maybe, to get away from his mother, though he couldn't have known why he was doing it then.

"Well anyway, after my teacher said, 'Never tell anybody you are from Arkansas,' I never did tell anyone where I had been born and grown up — (Sometimes I just said, 'Oh, I'm from out west.') — or about riding Bob into those holly fields I liked so much (and, certainly, not about the way the family lost them) — or much about myself at all. I never let anyone get close. Never even told your father much and never asked many questions of him.

"And I made good money in Chicago and later in Oklahoma City when they offered me that big job. Like all the others in the family, my time had come to travel around. Oklahoma City (where your father came backstage to meet me after a show) and Enid and later after the talkies came in and my playing days were over, to Texas, to San Antone where your father worked 'til the Crash came and he lost everything, his job and his mind. And after your father was gone, back to Arkansas to sit in the Little Green House, that shack without any plumbing, and be blue.

"So it's no wonder that, though I didn't like traveling much, I finally took off with Robby in the De Soto for Texas under a full moon that your Uncle Lloyd said was made of money. Took off even though I had to leave you behind with your grandmother and Daddy and you were only two. 'Look at the moon and wish on it,' Lloyd said. 'When you drive into Texas under that moon, wish on it again! Down there that moon will be made of hundred-dollar bills.'"

Chapter Six
Beatrice

Wishing wasn't getting, my mother always said. Life for her and Robby
was hard in Texas. Both of them worked ten- to twelve-hour days. But they
did at least have work there — Robby managed Cage's store — and it was a
cage for him, all right — and my mother taught music in the schools — and
bought what they needed and my mother sent money back to Arkansas
for me. And packages filled with such thrilling presents — sailor dresses
and giant Easter bunnies and dolls with real hair — that it seemed to me
they couldn't have come from the warmhearted but sorrowful mother I
remembered, but from some queen.

"Dear Mama," I wrote as soon as I could form the letters, for I had to
reach her. "Thank you for the presents. I made you a picture." From as long
as I can remember I had loved crayons and colored pencils, the discoveries I
made with them on drawing paper, that red and blue made purple and that if
I added pink I had what the Crayola box called Magenta. (I loved the color
and the name!) And that favorite combinations — pink and orange, lilac
and spring green, with a touch of blue — soothed any pain.

With these same crayons and pencils, sprawled out with tablet in front
of me on the cool linoleum of our dining porch floor, I learned to make my
letters early and called out to Nella, usually in the kitchen, who told me
which ones to put together for every word I wanted to write. "How do you
spell Dear?" "How do you spell Mama?" "How do you spell Thank?"

I wrote to my mother before I was three. And I drew and drew.

Never stopped no matter what anybody said about the pictures. (When
I was in school I never had a teacher who liked them much.) And consider
myself lucky to be able to make a modest living by teaching art.

But now I write about my mother instead of to her. Always long distance
— from my early years I thought of her as "the long distance mother." She
became a person that no matter how many letters I wrote, until her extreme
old age, even when we lived together under the same roof, I could seldom
reach. I wanted her to be happy. (She lived with so much yearning.) I
wanted the world to know about her. I wanted her dreams to come true.

If I don't tell you about her and Robby and all the others, who will?

If no one speaks of them, they will be forgotten.

My childhood country taught me that the links we have to one another
should be fluid, but visible. Shimmering like rays of light, looping us
together.

And yet also making space for journeys.

"That moon," my Uncle Lloyd had said, "will be made of money."

The moon is about all I remember of my first trips down to South Texas along the Hug-the-Coast. The moon and the dark water lapping across the beach. We traveled at night and I remember the dark nights and, at the same time, the big moon hung over us, illuminating the water and my Uncle Lloyd saying, "Look at the moon, honey, and make a wish on it." Lloyd was the businessman in the family, not one of the builders. I don't know why he was with us. Maybe he was just along for the ride, just coming for a visit. (Uncle Roy and Grandpa — Merrill and Merrill, their stationery read — were the contractors for all of the bridges that made possible the first unbroken highway along the coast.)

In answer, Aunt Ola who sat in the back seat with me on her lap next to Uncle Roy, said, "I do believe that moon is made of money."

Uncle Lloyd said to me then, "Do you see the Texas moon, honey? Wish for dolls and dresses and nice things!" "Oh Sis," he went on, "wish for a silver fox stole that you can wrap around you on stage before you play the piano. Wish for a big ring."

I could see the ring Lloyd wished for glittering on my mother's middle finger as she struck the keys. Yet all the time he spoke, I silently protested his invocations. An end to sorrow, it seemed to me, was the thing to wish for, not things.

"'Oh Sis, wish for a grand piano.'"

She would like that, I guessed, and when I thought about it afterwards, I knew the music she might have made on one would have eased her pain. But could even that I wondered release her truly? Who would have heard the music and where would she have made it? In Ingleside? That smelly little town?

Years later, when I remembered her playing the baby grand in the community house where she gave her spring recitals, oleander and field flowers delivered by pickups from Robby's store literally by the truck load to the stage, I realized that places like Ingleside had the most need to hear her music, and even if that weren't true, she heard it, and that everything somehow heard it, that the Gulf wind carried it to the bay and cruising seagulls, and that everything around us absorbed and trembled with it, town whittlers who sat all day on the bread box outside the IGA store and then disappeared into lonely rooms in sagging frame houses, to tots who in the afternoons had ridden their trikes up and down a cracked sidewalk, and then cried over their dinners and had been put fitfully to bed, to refinery workers outside in the blazing sun through all the daylight hours and asleep at night by nine in chairs next to their radios, to all the dogs and cats running loose, to the sap in the castorbean and salt cedar trees.

Maybe even the ghost of Annie Laurie heard it. And the wee ones that danced for Louise back in the woods, far away from the coast. In my mind those fey beings forever flitted around my mother. Protecting her? I considered that. Perhaps protecting us all.

2

Sometimes, without asking permission or telling anyone, I rode my bike through the main street of town and out of it, and then turned on a dirt road that I knew led toward the bay and the place where the shrimp boats were docked, the wind so fierce sometimes it was hard to steer — but I kept on going, and one day as the sky blackened, I knew I might be caught in rain and even more wind. When I got to the smelly bay, the little strip of sand before it, I parked the bike and sat down to sketch the boats and the water.

But I had really come there to shake off all that seemed to hold me down in life, Louise's sorrow, and Robby's (about which I will soon tell you) to be one with the elements — the sand and sky, the air and water — and to be taken back into the creation of things.

Sometimes when I was there I thought about my father.

"If you are a ghost," I said, "come to me here." (I wanted to add, "Here, where I am part of all the world and at the same time, alone.") But he never did.

"Oh, all right," I said, "maybe you aren't dead. Maybe you are just off somewhere. I'll just have to see you in my mind." And I tried to visualize him, but on that day when the sky blackened saw only that and the bay water before me, then a gull swooping down. For a moment I thought he might strike.

He didn't. But after that day, the bay, like so many places where we retreat, was not just a place of solace for me, but also, sometimes a place of dread.

Chapter Seven
Beatrice

Losses

Where had the fairies been when Lloyd, our moneymaker (and the only one) stumbled down a path toward a fishing lake and right into his death? I was a teen-ager, living with Robin and Nella, when that happened, when we got the call.

He had meant to go fishing. Fishing was what he did to get away from trying to pull more and more money in to win Jewell, who couldn't stand to have him touch her, and who couldn't seem to love him in any way at all. He had married her young (they were both sixteen) — had built up his wholesale candy and liquor business to take care of her — though they had been for years divorced.

I had heard about his going to this lake many times; going there was what he did when he had decided not to go on a binge instead. This time he wasn't drinking. After his last quarrel with Jewell he had some, yes, but then had pulled himself together, and gone north, driven up into the Ozarks proper to the White River where he turned off Route Seven and wound up into more hills on a dirt road and then stopped when he saw to one side a clear tributary, that fed into a lake which rested at the bottom of a treacherous trail. He stumbled — who knows why? — maybe because his eye was on the water — and fell a hundred feet and hit his head finally on a large boulder.

We know he wasn't drinking because, when they found him, there were no cans or bottles on the path — or in his tackle box or in the car, which he had parked on the dirt road up the way. He had been trying to get to water known for both trout and bass. I remember him talking about the lake when I was a little girl. "It's perfect," I can hear him saying — "perfect for fly fishing and has the best bass in the country, but it's a little hard to get to. As soon as I can get out from under the business a little, it's where I aim to go."

They said he had been dead only a little while when they found him — a couple of honeymooners who were staying at the lodge just off Route Seven and the White River.

He was fifty-three-years-old and left all he had to his son and to his ex-wife Jewell. His will said he expected her to give half of what she had to his mother if she outlived him. But Jewell never gave my grandmother anything.

I can still hear my mother saying, "That would have made him so unhappy." Lloyd, after all, was our provider, the one person in the family who always brought goods home.

God knows Lloyd needed protection. Had his protectors perhaps thought he would be better off out of this world?

2

And what were they thinking or where had they been the day the judge, who was Blanche's husband (a member of the family you might say) ruled against Lyman Roy who had forgotten to pay the taxes on the property?

Louise always said if we had had another judge things would have gone differently, that Blanche — "Old Hatchet Face" Lyman Roy always called her (and she knew that!) — had it in for him.

Anyway, that had happened without any protectors coming to our aid. Lyman Roy had been lost in a dream some way — the dream of his "temple" maybe, looking up too far through its skylights or shouting Hallelujahs in its big round room. Drunk or dreaming or both, that's what Lyman Roy, everyone said, had probably been. Nobody knew for sure. He disappeared for weeks at a time and nobody really knew if he was off on a job (sometimes he really was) or at the racetrack, or on a bender. But it was during one of these periods that the final notice had come for payment on the property. He had ignored the earlier ones and wasn't around to open this last.

Louise said this time he had come up the hill empty handed and looking very serious. (Sometimes when he came back he brought a sack of groceries with him and sang.) "I was on the porch," she said, "rocking. I had been rocking and talking to Ola for half the afternoon, and I was just rocking and looking through the trees at a little half moon, plain as can be though it was still daytime, when I saw Lyman Roy coming up the hill, moving slowly, long-faced and quiet — not grinning as he sometimes did when he returned like this — sober through and through. I got up then and went in the house to tell Ola and your grandmother that he was coming. 'Set another plate,' I said, 'I just saw Roy coming up the hill.' Your grandmother was frying the salmon cakes we all liked so much on the fired up wood stove, the cakes she rolled in cracker crumbs and beaten egg yolks and chili peppers. Your Aunt Ola was dishing up soup bowls of butter beans. When she spoke, I thought she was going to drop the one in her hand. 'Roy's here?'

"'In the flesh,' he said, coming through the kitchen door.

"'Oh,' Ola said, looking straight at him. 'This time I thought you were never coming home.'

"He smiled just a little. 'I had a job,' he said. 'I had to make a little money.' And from his pocket he pulled a hundred-dollar bill. She went to him then and touched his face and he kissed her.

"He told her he had been on a bridge job way off the south fork of the Mill Creek Road, way past The Church of the Morning Star. He said he never stayed away long unless he was on a job. 'I figured you all knew that. I didn't have a phone.'

"When we took our places at the table out on the dining porch, Daddy at one end and Mama near the kitchen on the other, Robby and I on one side by the back windows and Ola and Lyman on the other, we were all pretty quiet. And then, unexpectedly, Lloyd came in with a present, a black silk blouse with a matching scarf (the scarf had little pink roses on it) he had picked up for your grandmother — he had just come back from a buying trip for his business and stopped by to see us before going home — and she got up, all excited and kissed him after she opened her present and got him a chair.

"'Well,' he said, squeezing in next to Lyman. 'I see you're home.'

"The day had been hot. I noticed his white shirt had perspiration stains. I looked away and over my shoulder out the back windows at the big ball of fire the sun made as it went down over our dusty trees and the mountain in town.

"Your Uncle Lyman nodded and took a salmon cake from the plate as it was passed around. And then cornbread and a heap of slaw. 'Has anyone told you the news?' Lloyd asked him.

"'What news is that?'

"Lloyd's face was getting redder and redder and it was covered with perspiration from more than the heat of the afternoon. I could tell he was really furious with his brother. 'That while you were gone we lost the property in Pike County. The taxes which we all thought you had paid were long past due.'

"Your uncle didn't answer, but went white. 'I looked and looked for the papers, Lyman,' Ola finally said, 'and after a long time of rummaging around, found them in the bin under your desk, stuck in an old book — the one with the horse on the cover. The payment came due before you — ' She stopped then because she never liked to speak about what he did — 'before you disappeared.'

"'Why, I took care of that,' your Uncle Lyman said. 'I'm sure I sent the money off back in June.'

"'No, you didn't, Lyman,' Ola said. 'I looked through your checkbook.'

"'Well, I can pay it now. Maybe it came due when I was caught up in those big plans.'

"'It's too late, Roy,' Daddy said. 'If it weren't, Lloyd would have taken care of it. A court ruling has come down. The acreage is gone.'

"'What judge was on the bench?' Lyman asked. But he knew. 'Old Hatchet Face's man?'

"'Lyman!' Mama said. Blanche, who neither your Uncle Lyman nor I ever had any use for, had always been her favorite niece.

"I couldn't take it anymore. 'He's a son of a bitch!' I yelled and got up and left the table to go back to rock on the porch. I despised the whole family, but I was more furious at Blanche and her good-for-nothing husband than I could ever be at Lyman Roy and if either of them had been present I would have lifted my bowl of hot butter beans and thrown them over their heads."

Louise became very worked up even when she told this story. Robby's version was another thing. Unlike Louise, he hadn't a lot of use for Lyman Roy, mostly I think because Lyman Roy never gave him the kind of attention he wanted, and also because Lyman Roy was close to Daddy with whom he hardly had a relationship at all. He said his oldest brother never had a grain of sense about money. Not even enough to open his bills.

"I was present at the meal," Robby told me when I asked, "but I didn't say a word, just stared at Roy in disgust. He had been dreaming of building a church — can you imagine your Uncle Lyman in a church? — off on a cloud, and drunk half the time, and because of that, he lost the land that would have given us a future. Do you know he said to me one time, 'Rob, it's a mistake to get caught up in owning things, and anyway, when it comes to land, it's a lie. The land owns us, not the other way round.' He was drunk and crazy."

"It was the year of the drought," Louise told me later. "Everyone had lost crops. Poor Lyman, he was after Heaven when he and all of us needed somewhere good to live on Earth."

"Maybe we would have had it if you had asked," I told her. "You should have asked the fairies. 'Give me somethin.' When you see a fairy, that's what you have to say."

"Well, I was too awe struck to ask anything," Louise said. "But Robby, I think if he had seen those spirits instead of me, Robby would have asked. Shy as he is about some things, for something he really wants, he always does speak up."

After she told me this, I wondered if Robby saw fairies, too. But when once I asked he said, "As far as I know, your mother is the only one in this family who sees things." He said the closest he had ever come to seeing fairies was when he saw Ola, who would have made a large one, dressed up as an angel on a stage out in New Mexico in Mrs. Lucas' Christmas play. And he went on to tell me about that.

Chapter Eight
Robin

"Mrs. Lucas gave me her things. She said she wanted me to be the shepherd boy in the Christmas play — not just any shepherd boy, but the one who meets the brightest angel, the one the angel tells about the King of Love — so that he will believe and who gives him her crown.

"Mrs. Lucas loved plays. I never understood how she could have married a rancher. On every holiday she put on a play, used all the ranch hands and even Old Juan the night watchman (he was at least seventy) and Fat Linda the cook. She'd dress a lot of us up in her clothes, and she had all these costumes from the time before she married Mr. Lucas (he'd been dead for years, I guess), but I got the best ones — her beige chiffon dress, which she said she'd worn in Scotland draped over me like a robe and the sparkling tiara that made the angel so bright and that she offered it as if it was Jesus' crown.

"At first Louise wanted the part of the angel, but was happy when she found out she couldn't have it because Mrs. Lucas asked her to play the piano all through the pageant, right from the beginning to the end, 'The King of Love My Shepherd Is' to 'Silent Night.' Mrs. Lucas got your Aunt Ola who had come out on a visit to take the part of the angel. Can you imagine that? Said it was all right that Ola was a little plump and not a blonde. "Heaven is full of dark-haired angels," she told me. "And I'll bet some hefty ones, too. We'll just have to get someone strong to pull her strings."

"Oh, your fat Aunt Ola. She was on the heavy side even then. But after Mrs. Lucas got through with her, it didn't matter. Mrs. Lucas put her in a silver tent dress so you couldn't tell what shape she was. And she looked royal.

"After the play was over, Mrs. Lucas let me keep her tiara and I wore it all the time. Had it on my head the day I slid off the stable roof. An angel at Christmastime had come to me with everything that sparkled — never mind that it was really just Ola. 'Here, I give you my brightness,' was the line the angel said (Mrs. Lucas wrote the script) 'Take it as a sign.'

"I thought it might mean I could fly like the angel, at least in my mind. I always did somehow think I could fly. I had dreams that I could, and never mind that I didn't do it the time that by accident I fell off our Arkansas roof. Oh I knew I couldn't really do it, that no one in a human body flies. I knew your Aunt Ola went up in the air during that performance at the Matador Ranch because Mrs. Lucas had her hooked up to wires and a machine! And that big brute of a man had to turn it.

"My arms were in casts all winter — just as they had been back in Arkansas that other time, were broken in the elbows, in the same places. But I didn't mind too much because I was excused from writing up school lessons — I never liked school or lessons of any kind — and lots of days didn't even have to go, but just stayed home with Mama who helped in the kitchen with some of the cooking, but who mostly just sewed and sewed. And she taught me to sew some. I could do simple stitches on cloth even though I couldn't move my arms. Mama made all the women's dresses. And even some costumes for the show.

"'God knows,' she always said, 'Mrs. Lucas needs new ones. The old ones look like rags. In a good wash, they'd fall apart.' But a good wash, she said, was something they'd never had.

"'Antiques,' Mrs. Lucas always called them. 'They're antique costumes.'

"New Mexico was a new world to me. I wanted to stay there and was disappointed when Daddy said your mother was better and that we were going home."

2

"Daddy was distant from me. Didn't understand a thing about me. Never tried much. We never could get along. But maybe it's natural to be closer to your mother than to your father.

"Seems like Daddy was always at me. Wanting me to work alongside those uncouth ranch hands digging ditches, driving posts in the ground, putting up fences, hammering boards together. And before I fell from the roof I did all that and didn't mind it. Learned to carpenter young and could go on doing it even after I broke my arms and they were good and mended. But couldn't take being around those crude men.

"They were always talking about sex, only that wasn't the word they used. 'Hell, I'd just tell her to take her clothes off. And then I'd fuck her.' I heard one of them say that. And then another telling about how he had done it.

"I was just a kid, but I knew what they meant. And I hated them for it. 'Don't talk like that!' I blurted out to the one who was the loudest, and he had it in for me ever after and called me 'sissy' or 'Geraldine.' But I hated him for using that word.

"I knew what it meant and I knew that's what Daddy did to Mama. Oh, I'd hear her crying some nights from the next room. 'No, Daddy, no. Get away from me, Daddy. Daddy, don't do it!' And then I'd hear her scream

a little. 'Daddy stop it! Oh please stop it.' And I'd hear their bed a rockin'
because he was going on and on.

"And I'd hate him. Yes, hate him, my own father. Mama always said all
men were nasty and that he was just a man. But she knew I'd be different.
That I would never be like that and I told myself I was never going to be.

"And I didn't want to be outside with those crude men (Oh your Uncle
Roy was no better than them that way.) 'Don't make me go out there,' I'd say
to Daddy — scared as I was, I often just spoke up — 'I don't like those men
and one of them calls me names.' I liked to be in the house helping mama
and Mrs. Lucas — she let me play for a long time in the attic with her old
things and once had me help her recover an antique chair.

"She had brought it all the way from Scotland, a beautiful curved thing
with carved lion heads at the end of the arms, but all tattered, the material
that covered it all torn. But one day, Mrs. Lucas took me to town with her
to find some new material and let me pick it out, a heavenly deep blue
velveteen, and when we got it back to the ranch, she let me cut it — Mama
had taught me how and said I had a good eye for measurement — and
together, we tacked it in. And it was a gorgeous thing.

"Then Mrs. Lucas told me she was going to make a present of it to Mama,
and that she wanted me to present it on Mama's birthday which was a special
day in new Mexico because it was the Day of the Dead, November two,
when the whole ranch, because it had so many Mexican workers, took off.
And that I wasn't to talk about it until then, that it was to be a secret.

"I can never remember being so excited. I had never had such a secret.
And I'd never seen a piece of furniture as beautiful as that chair. I couldn't
believe we were going to own it. Or that I had helped make it look like it did
and could tell Mama.

"I couldn't wait 'til her birthday.

"When it came, Fat Linda set up an altar on a wooden kitchen bench for
her dead father, covered it with a hand embroidered cloth and made bread
to put on it and cake (but let me eat a little.) She made a birthday cake for
Mama, angel food, Mama's favorite with a thick vanilla icing. She had never
made an angel cake before she said — she let me spoon out some batter
— but thought it would turn out all right because Mrs. Lucas had given her
the recipe.

"'Will your father come and eat the bread and cake?' I asked her.

"'He might come and eat a little,' she told me. 'We'll see tomorrow.' She
would leave the altar up all night she said. He would probably come after the
big party in the dining room to honor my mother's birthday was over, maybe
even after we were all asleep.

"What a night! I can never remember being so excited. Everyone got all dressed up. Your grandmother wore a blue dress she had made the exact color of the chair, (periwinkle she called it) — only she didn't know about the chair, didn't know she was going to get it!

"Mama looked so pretty — she was little, you know, petite — her hair on top of her head, her mother's cameo on her collar — she had colored the gray in her hair an auburn brown and she even wore rouge. And she was smiling. People always said that she was serious, that she didn't smile much. Well, how could she with her life so hard? I always remember her smiling, I guess, because she so often smiled at me. But nobody could have said she looked serious this night.

"When Mrs. Lucas said, 'Happy birthday, Nella!' she lit up like a sparkler. And Fat Linda's boys had some of those — because of the Day of the Dead.

"I saw them playing with them on the porch and the rain on the other side of it just a pouring down — Lord, what a rainy night, the whole ranch a mud hole by morning — and I heard Linda call them in.

"They had their dinner in the kitchen and left some of it on the bench with the bread and cake for their grandfather. Linda also put a bottle of beer out for him, a package of Camel cigarettes and a cup of black coffee. She said you had to give the dead what they liked, that they weren't going to improve their habits just because they had taken off for another world.

"I saw all this when I went into the kitchen with Mrs. Lucas to bring out Mama's cake. I thought it was all loco, that Linda and some of the other Mexicans were loco, just off, you know in the *cabeza*, but I didn't hate them the way I did the ranch hands, those big uncouth men. Linda and her boys and aunts and uncles who came to visit, her whole family as far as I could tell were all polite, soft spoken and kind. But strange to me in their ways. This was all a long time ago. I was no more than nine or ten. I had never been around any Mexican people.

"Maybe that's why I remember Linda and her boys so clearly giving the boys' dead grandfather part of their dinner. And before with their sparklers on the porch.

"At the dinner table, Mrs. Lucas made a speech saying how much help Mother and Daddy and the whole family — Roy and Ola had finally come out — had been to her, that she was glad that Colonel Lucas had bought the ranch and kept up with his friend, Annie's family. Colonel Lucas had once been a suitor of Daddy's mother, but in Fiona Lucas finally married a woman young enough to be his daughter.

"Since your mother had to be in a dry climate for a while, it was a good thing for us that the Lucas family was in New Mexico. We heard Mrs. Lucas say in her speech that we all needed each other. And I guessed that was true.

"After Mrs. Lucas' speech, she and I brought out the cake and oh, how Mama smiled and blew out all the candles!

"And after dinner, Louise played for all of us in the parlor. Chopin, my favorite of all the composers she liked, and then that piece called 'Romance' by Rubenstein that she's always played all the time. And then, for Daddy and all of us and Mr. Lucas, too, 'Annie Laurie.'

"And then Mrs. Lucas brought out the chair. She said, 'Robby went to town with me to pick out the fabric and cut it to fit and then the two of us tacked it in. And I want you to keep it always to remember your time with Fiona Lucas by, and Mama just beamed, and Louise and Ola and Roy, too, but Daddy sure didn't. And Mrs. Lucas had honored his mother, who had once been her rival, as I would always honor mine. After that it never seemed right to me that finally Daddy got the chair."

Chapter Nine
Robin

"No sooner was Mama's party and all that excitement over and it was Thanksgiving. Fat Linda made turkey tamales the very next day and I liked them more than I'd liked the Thanksgiving dinner. Seems it had rained ever since Mama's birthday. I had a cold that she was afraid would go into bronchitis or worse — my lungs were not much better than your mother's; when I was little I had pneumonia. So I got to stay inside. Mama taught me to crochet and to sew and I made potholders for Linda for Christmas.

"The day after the party I got up early, and went to the kitchen early because I wanted to see what Linda's dead father had eaten from all she and the boys put out. Nothing. Nothing that I could see. But Linda claimed he had drunk some from the mug of beer, that there wasn't as much in it.

"'Course there wasn't,' your mother said when I told her about it. 'After it sits in the open air for an hour or two liquid evaporates.'

"Mrs. Lucas said she had a better explanation, much as she respected the dead and the customs of all the Mexican workers on her ranch. Old Juan, the night watchman, one of Linda's uncles — most of the workers were related — probably had drunk the beer, Mrs. Lucas said. She had never seen him resist an open bottle no matter who it was for. But he might have stopped, scared, when he realized it was for a ghost.

"That satisfied my curiosity and since I saw the sun was out I asked Mrs. Lucas if she thought I could go riding on my pony even though I had a cold. But she said it was too muddy, so I stayed in and watched her paint a china plate (Mama and the rest of the family was off shopping in town) and finally she gave me a plate and a paint brush and let me begin a flower. She said maybe I would want to give it to Mama for Christmas and as things turned out I did. Kept it a secret, and every time Mama was out, painted a little more on it.

"Hardly any time had passed when all kinds of preparations were being made for Christmas. Mrs. Lucas was in the attic digging out old costumes and in the afternoons, instead of painting china, worked on the Christmas play.

"'Robby,' she told me, 'I want you to be the Shepherd Boy. Do you think you can memorize lines?'

"'Yes,' I said, though I wasn't sure I could. I was scared to death of the idea of standing on a stage in front of people and saying anything at all. But at the same time, I wanted to be in the play. 'Yes,' I said, 'I could learn them. What would I get to wear?'

"She took me up in the attic then and we went through all her old
evening dresses and jewelry and all the costumes she'd ever used for one of
her plays. I'd never seen anything like all that. For weeks I wanted to go to
the attic every day. And Mrs. Lucas took me there, and there she taught me
the lines I was going to have to say.

"'You see,' she said, 'in the play an angel chooses a boy to tell about The
King of Love.' That was the baby Jesus. 'And gives that boy a gift so he'll
always have faith. He wants to talk to God. And then in a poem he does.'

"A verse from an old hymn that Mrs. Lucas had altered a little was what
I had to learn to say. And I learned it and I practiced every afternoon in the
attic.

"And I loved it. But was scared to death anyway."

3

"When Christmas Eve came, I was trembling. That was the night when
we did the play. Then Mrs. Lucas was there and she put her arm around me
and said, 'Robby, do you remember your lines? Do you remember the prayer
you are to say?'

"I shook my head because all at once I couldn't remember.

> *The King of Love my shepherd is*
> *Whose kingdom faileth never*
> *But He is mine and I am His*
> *This night, now and forever*

"Her voice trembled as she said the words. 'Remember, Robby, before you
say that, the King of Love says: 'You and your brothers keep the sheep and
I keep you.' (The King of Love's lines were to be delivered off stage by your
Uncle Roy on a microphone. We all hoped he would stay sober.) 'Yes, now
I remember,' I said. 'You are a good boy, Robby,' she said. 'The real King of
Love is with you.'

"And I hoped so. Anyway, Linda's boys, Michael and Gabriel were with
me — we were all shepherds in the play (even though Linda had named
them after angels) — and both of them sang a song in Spanish and English,
three long verses. Each had a verse by himself, then sang the last one
together. I didn't get a verse because I told Mrs. Lucas I wouldn't be in the
play at all if I had to sing. 'I can't sing,' I told her, 'if I have to sing I won't be
in the play.' After Michael and Gabriel finished singing, Old Juan came on

the stage — he was supposed to be their grandfather — to take them away. I waved to them and then I was on the stage alone and heard Roy's voice say, 'You keep the sheep and I will keep you.' Roy sounded all right. I knew Mama would be happy that he at least put off getting drunk until after the show. And then Ola in her sparkling dress and Mrs. Lucas' old tiara came down on wires from the top of the barn. And she said to me, 'You have been chosen. I give you my brightness,' and took off her tiara and put it on my head. 'Wear this and go and show yourself to your brothers.'

"'The King of Love my shepherd is,' I began. My voice trembled. I went blank and stopped. Then I heard Mrs. Lucas prompting me and I remembered our time in the attic when she would read me old stories and tell me about her girlhood in Scotland."

Chapter Ten
Robin

"'I liked the church plays, Robby. And I liked to go to the theater festival in Edinburgh. Our school went to half a dozen performances every year as a group. And oh, we saw some wonderful things. Shakespeare every year and the ones I liked the best were the fairy plays, (or that's the way I thought of them.) 'The Tempest,' and 'Cymbaline' and 'A Midsummer Night's Dream.' I was shy as a girl — would you believe that, Robby? But the stories I saw acted out had such an effect that I had to be in one. And so I worked up the courage to audition for our church play at Christmastime and I was accepted in the chorus and the year after that as soloist and a reader, and I did well enough to make me think I could try out for the Shakespeare our school was putting on in the spring.

"'And would you believe that in 'Macbeth' I got two witches' speeches as well as the role of the principal Moving Bush? And I liked doing that so much that I auditioned every year. And I got more and more parts, but really I was always more interested in the whole production, the whole story, than in doing any one part, and by the time I was through school, I directed the church plays.'

2

"It came back to me in a flash how she told me all that and the way her eyes shown as they looked right into mine — her eyes were the softest gray-blue — all crinkled at their leathery corners, (her skin nearly brown as a Mexican she was out in the sun so much.)

"I don't know what came over me. I lost my fear. And instead of saying the rest of 'The King of Love' I started over and sang. I had a clear soprano voice and often sang when I thought no one could hear me.

> *The King of Love my shepherd is*
> *Whose kingdom faileth never*
> *But he is mine and I am his*
> *This night, now and forever*

"I sang right to the audience. I couldn't really see their faces, but I knew many people I knew were there, Daddy and all the ranch hands, even the ones I detested, even the one who called me 'sissy' and 'Geraldine.' They were all there, all those men and their poor families and people I didn't know but saw on the street in Clayton. Mrs. Lucas was known all over that part of New Mexico for her plays. I sang right to all the people. Afterwards, Mama said I should have voice lessons and that I should sing in the choir."

3

"That was the most thrilling Christmas I can ever remember. We even had snow. It started falling right after the curtain came down. After the play, Mrs. Lucas gave a big party. Everyone on the ranch was there, though most came late after the midnight Mass at the Catholic church in town. Linda served more of her tamales and had also prepared a chicken *mole* which none of us had eaten before — nobody said anything bad to Linda about it because they wanted to be polite — and *sopapillas* with honey which I had never had before either (but I liked them so much I ate three.) And there was a band and dancing. Your mother did the Mexican hat dance with me, and she showed me how to polka.

"All the hands drank beer and *Margaritas* (your Uncle Roy drank whiskey from a flask he kept in his pocket) and Mama wouldn't let me have any, but when we went in the living room to open our presents — just our family and Mrs. Lucas, I was allowed a glass of champagne. Mrs. Lucas had it just for us, though she knew Mama wouldn't take any and didn't want me to. 'Now Nella, I'm giving him just a spoonful because it's a party.' But I didn't need it to get high.

"I didn't need it to go up on the roof either. When the excitement of Christmas died down, I helped Mrs. Lucas put up all the costumes and sometimes she let me stay on in the attic just to play.

"Stacks of books, histories and geographies filled the shelves of an old bookcase on one of the attic walls. I'd never liked reading much. Daddy was always reading. If he wasn't at a job his nose was in a newspaper or a book. I never remember him making conversation with Mama, though I know he and Roy were close and when they went places together, as they did sometimes, he talked to your mama. I came to think that readers separated themselves from people. But these books drew me to them because they were so big and then when I opened one I saw it was full of maps and pictures.

"When Mrs. Lucas found me with it, she said, 'Why, Robby, that's my favorite Geography,' and she sat down next to me in the crude window seat where I had perched myself and opened the book to the middle and a gigantic map of the world. 'Just look, Robby,' she said. 'Here we are.' And she put her finger by the yellow spot that I guessed was New Mexico. Then she moved her hand across the map all the way up to Scotland. 'This is where I came from and where your grandmother came from. And one day, Robby, you should see it.'

"'But,' I said to her, 'it's across all that water.' And I ran my hand over a whole half page that was blue. The book was blue, too, 'my big blue Geography' Fiona Lucas said. I told Fiona then — and I thought of her sometimes as Fiona and not just as Mrs. Lucas — that I was afraid of water, had been ever since my cousins dunked me under Lake Catherine when we went swimming there. Your grandmother's niece's children. Oh, they were mean girls. 'I wouldn't want to cross the water on a boat,' I told Mrs. Lucas. 'No matter,' she said. 'You'll get over your fear,' (but I never did). 'You should see the wide world.' Then she pulled another book off one of the shelves and showed me pictures of aeroplanes. 'Who knows, maybe one day you'll get around the world in a plane.'

"When she left and I was alone, I pretended I was in the play all over and said my lines and sang my song. And I thought about what Fiona Lucas had said to me about seeing Scotland and the world and daydreamed that I might somehow do it in an aeroplane.

"Then one day I climbed the ladder that led up to a skylight. When I got to the top, I saw that the glass opened like a window and that I could get out on the roof. The snow we had on Christmas had melted, but the roof was still wet and slick in places with icy patches.

"I played out my part all over. It was a windy day. I can still hear the wind singing and I sang too. I sang and sang. And was thrilled, Beatrice, to hear my own singing. I thought there was nothing I couldn't do. I stretched out my arms wide and ran a little, and then began to slide and before I knew it, I was gone.

"I hadn't really set out to do this — that was just a story your mother told. You know how she tells stories. I knew a boy couldn't fly, no matter what I had been thinking about.

"But once I was in the air, I tried to lead with my arms and fell on my knees and elbows right into the wagon Juan had parked by the side of the barn and then tumbled off that to the ground. Old Juan's blankets, which covered the wagon, softened my first landing a little. But I was scared I can tell you, and I thought Mama might die, she threw such a fit.

"But Mrs. Lucas stayed calm and called the doctor in Clayton and Linda carried me to the couch in the living room where your mother practiced the piano. She hadn't heard the commotion I guess. The whole room rumbled with the music — but then it stopped and your mother's mouth and eyes both opened wide. 'Why, what has happened?' she asked Linda. 'Your brother was playing on the roof, maybe thinking he had wings,' Linda said. Well, that's how that story got started.

"Before I knew it, the ambulance was there with the doctor and by the next day, both my arms were in casts. And the dreary winter stretched on and on. I spent a lot of it in bed.

4

"And those were dull days — but Mama made them a little better by giving me needlework to do, crocheting and embroidery. My fingers could move and I could work the needles even with my arms in a cast. So I stayed more or less busy. And Mrs. Lucas came to show me more in the big Geography and, sometimes, to read to me from some of her old plays.

"One day she came in costume — a long, mauve, filmy gown with a scoop neck and puffy sleeves, and on her head she wore a crown, dried flowers: roses and fern and a purple field flower. She carried a shiny, deep purple fan. At this time Fiona Lucas must have been past 70; her straight gray hair hung loose just above her shoulders, and everything she wore looked almost as old as she.

"She turned around in front of my bed and said 'How do you like this, Robby?'

"And I said, 'Oh, I do. I do like it.'

"'Well, then, there's a dance that goes with it,' she told me. 'And a song.'

"And she twirled round and round — a fey thing who seemed only distant kin to the woman I had seen through my window out riding in a Western shirt and pants and moccasins early in the morning.

"Round and round she danced and she sang, too.

"And she said, 'Robby, come and I'll show you the steps. Your arms may be broken, but your feet are still lively. Come on. It isn't good for a boy to lie abed all day.'

"And I got up and she showed me what to do. 'We'll work on these steps,' she said, 'and by next Christmas we'll have a new entertainment for the show.'

"But we had no more than got started when there was a rapping at the door. And it was Daddy.

"'Fiona,' he said, 'excuse me, but we're breakin' some horses and I thought Robby might like to watch.'

"Sometimes I was just bold in front of him. 'Mrs. Lucas, is teaching me a dance,' I said. 'And a new song. We might use it in a show.' I knew I'd have to sit by the horse ring with all those crude men and I didn't want to go."

"'Well, Robby,' she said, squeezing my hand, 'it's good to learn how to handle horses too.'

"So that was that. I had to put on my clothes and go. I liked to go out and ride my pony beside Linda's boys, who shared a horse. And I didn't mind watching the men break the horses, though I felt sorry for the horses to tell the truth, sorrier than for the men who got thrown. But I hated the company I'd have to keep.

"'Why, Robby,' Mrs. Lucas said — and she was still a sight to see — 'take off that long face. We'll learn more of the dance tomorrow. Today you find out more about how to ride.'

5

"If I had really wanted to know a lot more about riding, I wouldn't have needed lessons from any of those men. Your mother I thought knew everything there was to know. She didn't have Bob in New Mexico, but she rode every horse on the ranch and if she had wanted to, I'll bet she could have ridden in the rodeo. Her only interest in performing was on a stage, but, as soon as she was well enough, she was always off somewhere on horseback, and sometimes on a tear.

"The afternoon the men were breaking the horses, she came flying down the road toward us on a gray stallion.

"Daddy left me with Linda's boys in the front row of the stands while he went off to work in the barn. Then that filthy-mouthed hand came toward us though he hardly looked at Linda's sons.

"'Well, just look at who's here,' he said. 'If it isn't 'Geraldine.'"

"'Robin,' I shot back at him. 'Don't call me a girl's name.'

"'Well, Robin's a girl's name, too, I reckon. Did your Maw want a little lady? Or didn't she think you'd ever make a man?'

"'Most people call me Robby,' I almost whispered — after he shamed me I couldn't at first seem to make a full sound. But I could express myself. 'She didn't want me to have exactly the same name as my father, whose name is Robert,' I said. And I almost said she named me Robin because I was born early in the spring. (Mama always told me that during the first part of April she looked for robins, that they brought her luck, but I didn't want to tell this mean hand that.)

"'Is that so, Rob-in?' he mocked. 'Well, you don't seem to take to flying. I see you broke your wings.' He hooped and hollered over that.

"Your mother slid off her gray about then. She had overheard all of this. I thought she was going to take her riding whip and lash him across the face. But she didn't. She just gave him a look that did it, and she said, 'Isn't your name Giff?' He nodded. 'Thank you, Giff,' she told him. 'Mrs. Lucas will be interested in what you've just said to my brother.' Then she took my hand and said, 'Come on, Rob. You don't have to stay here with this uncouth son of a bitch.' And she lifted me up to the horse and put me on it in front of the saddle.

"And high and mighty, and pretty as you please, we rode back to the ranch house where Mama called out to Louise from the place where she was sewing in front of the fire. She wanted to pin the hem of the dress she was making and told her to take off her riding pants.

"'I just had a run-in with that s.o.b. Giff,' Louise said to Mama. 'Fiona ought to have him fired.'

"'Louise, watch your tongue,' Mama said, as your mother pulled the dress over her head.

"By this time, Mama was on her knees in front of your mother, pinning the hem.

"'Giff's mean,' your mother said, 'a mean son of a bitch, that's all you can make of him.'

"'Louise!' Mama said. 'Watch your mouth. And stand still.'

"'A son of a bitch,' Louise repeated, 'he said mean things to Robby.'

"'Watch what YOU say,' Mama nearly shouted.

"'I say 'Damn him to hell!'' your mother said, glaring at Mama. You know the look she has when hell rises in her, or maybe when she's taken down into it — that fixed stare. Then she said, 'Let me out of this rag.'

"'Louise, stand still,' Mama told her. 'And quiet your tongue.'

"But your mother was well under, deep in the underworld by this time. She stared at Mama and then at the fire as if she was seeing herself in the flame.

"'You've always wanted me to be ugly,' she said. 'And you never wanted me to have any fun or even any rest. You take everything away. (She didn't know then that finally Mama would take Bob away.)

"'Louise!' Mama whispered. 'You'd better be quiet.'

"'Your fault,' your mother repeated. 'I had a breakdown. Your fault we're here. Well, this is what I think of your rag!' And she tore the dress off of her, her eyes flaming, and threw it in the fire. And turned, and half-naked, ran out of the room and out of the house!

"I swear to God I'm telling you the truth.

"I've never seen such a look on your grandmother's face.

"It was just despair.

"I stood next to her trembling. 'I'm sorry, Mama,' I said. I saw the dress she had cut and stitched from material she bought with such hard-earned money burning in the fire. It was for a Valentine's party, lavender velveteen. 'I don't know what's the matter with Louise,' I stammered. 'Something happens to her.'

"Mama drew me to her. 'You're a good boy, Robby,' she said, 'the only really good child I had. The two grown boys, your brothers, are drunkards, and your sister's a hellion and I don't know why. And I can't talk to your father. But I can talk to you and you know what I say is true.'

"I helped her put her sewing things away and then I went upstairs.

"And for the first time in a long while took the twisting stairs up to the attic door and went in and looked up toward the skylight. I couldn't get up to it this time because the ladder had been taken permanently away. So I just stared up at it and looked at the blue sky through the clear pane, wishing. I loved my mother and it broke my heart to see her hurt. And I loved your mama, too, though I never knew where her wild streak or her meanness came from.

"But a lot of the time I wished I could break away from both of them — and from all the family. A lot of the time, I just wished I could be free."

Chapter Eleven
Robin

"That day I sure wasn't going to get out on to the roof. The whole family saw to it I didn't play on rooftops or even by myself much anymore. They found plenty for me to do. Chores inside and out even after we got back to Arkansas from New Mexico, which stayed so alive in my mind because I found my courage there and stepped into happiness, though I was, afterwards, also pushed into shame. (And I don't know if I can tell you about that. Sometime, maybe I'll try to, because it's a shame I can never forget.)

"They kept me busy for years, until I was through with high school, which I never liked much — and sent me down to Texas where Roy and Daddy had been building bridges, to run old man Cage's store. (They knew I was in no shape to do construction work and I was glad about that because I had never liked it and hated camping outside.) I was to get free rent — in the back of the place, and you know what that was like — a hundred dollars a month, plus anything I wanted from Cage's at cost, and credit at the IGA store. I was just eighteen-years-old and felt like I was serving a sentence, but I got used to it. And I made some changes in what Cage's carried, talked old man Cage into carrying a good line of furniture and a gift shop that sold Haviland china and showed him how it could be displayed, and it all sold. (The refinery women even asked me to come into their houses and arrange the furniture.) I was there ten years before your mother came.

"But you know about those Texas years. So I'm going to skip ahead to my leaving for the war, being sent to California and then out into the wide world. Across an expanse of blue, all right, bigger than any in Fiona Lucas' Geography! Over the big Pacific to Honolulu, which I knew when I first saw it had been waiting for me all my life.

"Oh, you know about those Ingleside years and how your mother and I worked there — she wearing out the pavement between the grammar school and high school teaching piano to all those refinery young'uns — seven in the morning 'til almost that time at night, and me in Cage's store from sunup 'til sundown, and sometimes way after. I worked in the store rearranging merchandise and on displays half the night sometimes. And you remember.

"But you don't know about how the world opened up for me after I enlisted in the Navy and went west. First to San Diego, where I was stationed for more than a year, and then, finally to the islands. The world, I found out, was mostly sea. Though I never, thank God, had to fight or even be on it. My broken arms kept me out of action. The Navy flew me to Waikiki.

"Before I left Ingleside, your mother took me to this woman who was a reader. Scotch-Irish, she said, and from three generations of women with second sight. She took me in a little room off her living room where your mother waited, and she sat me at a card table covered with purple cloth. Then from a drawer she took out a crystal ball, and for two or three minutes she just stared into the thing. When she had seen enough, she looked across at me and said, 'You'll be on the water in two places and one of them you'll have a chance for happiness. You won't be in battle. You won't fight on the water. Or even cross it on a boat.'

"And I never did. In San Diego and Honolulu, too, I was a storekeeper. That's what I knew how to do, what I had experience in and I didn't mind it (I even liked to play store as a child.) I couldn't be assigned to active duty because of my arms. So being in the service wasn't bad. I saw a lot that was new.

"In California, when I had a leave, I took a bus to Fresno and visited the man and his wife who used to be Cage's truck driver in the lumber yard that was attached to the store, so poor that they hardly had enough to eat and struck out to California for a new life and found it, and they drove me all around — to the wine country and to the redwood forest — I never saw anything like those big trees — and all through the farming country north and south of Santa Barbara, the strawberry fields, miles and miles of them just east of the coast.

"Then a year later in Honolulu, I ran into a fellow in my unit who was once Cage's bookkeeper — those people from the Coastal Bend in Texas scattered all over the world — and we had ourselves a time. We got twenty-four-hour Liberty, and those were hard to come by in the years just after Pearl Harbor. Honolulu was under strict watch.

"But we got a whole day away from the base. Stayed out for half of one night and the next day walked, spent the day walking, until finally we reached the top of a hill with the harbor and ocean — and the whole world it seemed spread before us. I forgot about the war.

"After that, when liberties came — they only gave us one or two others, we went to some of the beaches. And I had a girl, my girl, with me. (And what was that about? Oh, I'll have to tell you!) And once we were flown for supplies to the Big Island, and stopped at Maui just for a look on the way back.

"When I left Ingleside, I was afraid I was going to hell and instead I realized I had been living in hell and was on my way to heaven. When I look back now, I see California as a station on the way. And if it hadn't been for that accident that sent me back, and if you and your mother, and Mama who was still alive but getting old and wanting me to make a home for her and Daddy in Texas, hadn't been waiting for me there, I would never have returned."

Chapter Twelve
Beatrice

Robin wouldn't tell me more, so I said, "Tell me about her and what happened in Hawaii.'

But he couldn't, I could see that, not at first. He couldn't tell me much.

"What was her name?" I asked him. I thought that would be a beginning.

"Sharon Marie," he told me. "We were in a show together."

"What kind of show?" I wanted to know.

"One that the officers' wives put on," he said. "She was a captain's daughter. I had just been promoted to ensign. She was very sweet. She sang."

"Did you have scenes together? What was your part?"

"We had some songs in the same scene and we had to rehearse a lot. But once on a liberty we borrowed a car and drove halfway around the island to climb to the lookout at Makapu Lighthouse and were caught there in light mist and rain.

"But we didn't turn back. We had walked a long way up a narrow path, lush green on both sides and thick with ferns and flowers, some white ones as big as saucers, and we meant to reach the top. We were going for the view.

"When we came to the clearing, we saw the lighthouse and down below, the ocean — even in rain still blue — and a strip of what I took to be beach, except that it wasn't exactly anymore. Because it was a rainbow. Reflected light broken up through raindrops and somehow thrown against the sand. I had never seen such colors. Spring green – that really light, bright green with yellow in it. And turquoise, the same color as some of the water (in the places where it wasn't sapphire blue.) And indigo. And gold. The strip of color that curled around the mountains, red-gold fire! And Sharon leaned against me — her arm around my waist and mine over her shoulder — and gasped, and then whispered, 'Oh look! Oh, Rob — Rob — '

"And, Beatrice, suddenly — for just a second — I knew how we are all in it here. And I heard more than Sharon speaking to me. Somehow, and I don't know how — I hallucinated, maybe, or maybe I just don't remember this right — a rainbow had strung itself before me across this far beach at the base of some high hills.

"And said, 'Stay here. Why go back to trouble? To all that binds and hurts you? Stay here with the green hills and the blue water — the blue that makes up most of the world. And the broken, colored light.'

"Really, though I know I sound crazy, it seemed to say that — seemed to tell me — it was as if I could hear it tell me: 'This is happiness. This loves you.'

"Bea, for just a second, it was as if I could hear that said: 'All this loves you.'

"And: 'It's yours. Claim it.'

"I stepped forward then and felt myself slipping. Sharon grabbed me, held my arm. 'Robby,' she said, 'be careful. Don't go flying off.'"

Part II

Chapter Thirteen
Beatrice

He said for a long time he tried not to. How could he know that he was destined, seemed fated always to fall?

Was the promise of love and beauty too much for him?

After he became an ensign, he no longer clerked in, but managed the naval base store, and often picked up or delivered goods. And from all those years with Cage, he knew just how to do that. The job absorbed him, the job and being with Sharon Marie in the play.

"And I will tell you about it someday," he told me. "I promise. Until I had the accident it was all part of the best time I have ever known.

"Beatrice, it's something, just being here. And when I was with her, with Sharon, I really knew I was.

"She was a shimmering thing — small, but such a glow about her. From the first I felt it, saw it even — in the way she moved and spoke — before I ever watched her on a stage. I just always wanted to be near that. Wherever she was — even though I was afraid sometimes — I wanted to be.

"The miracle is that she wanted that, too.

"We were, you know, before the accident, in that officers' club play together. We had just the best time, (the best I'd had since I was in New Mexico with Fiona Lucas.) And one day I will tell you about it.

"Oh, I don't know why what happened happened. I swear I didn't will it. And this was before I started drinking. I didn't start drinking until the Navy gave me my discharge. I went back to Texas after.

"I wanted to stay there — I was afraid sometimes, but I wanted to claim my place. The world was so blue — all ocean and sky. That blue seemed all there was, and I was going right into it. I didn't see one of the turns there on Koko Head Road, which had one after another. I just went off, over the side."

Robby always stopped there. He said, after rescue and emergency treatment, the Navy sent him to a hospital back in San Diego where it rained all winter. For a while he kept in touch with Sharon, but after his discharge, he didn't return to her or to the place that had spoken to him of happiness and asked him to stay.

He left instead for Texas, where he made a home for Nella and Roy, who asked him to after they sold their place in Arkansas which had grown too hard for them to keep. A home goods store in San Antonio hired him to run it and later transferred him to a branch in Corpus Christi. The relocations took all his time and strength. He stopped writing to Sharon Marie.

But after a long silence from Hawaii, he did finally get a letter. Sharon wrote that her parents had introduced her to a family friend, a lieutenant, who had asked her to marry him. She missed Robin, but he didn't write anymore. She had always wanted her own home and family. She asked, "What should I do, Robby?"

He never answered her question, but if he had, he would have said that she should marry the naval officer her father had in mind for her and go on with the kind of life she had always known before.

Chapter Fourteen
Beatrice

I read somewhere that the blueness of the world and its oceans comes from the interior, steamed out of the Earth itself. Among our losses in the twentieth century was some of that blue — though from the far reaches of space, and from many of our globe's places (the beaches of Maui and Kauai and others) the loss is not yet noticeable. We've poured so much poison into what was once blue (and blighted or deleted much of the green along with it) that maybe the Earth doesn't breathe the way it used to and can't release the natural color from its center because it can't get its breath.

One way or another, most of us, I guess, are wounded as children, Robby, my mother and Nella and Roy before them, though I've never been clear on just how. I was no exception. Awful hurt in them, those first school years with Louise, my mother who I had thought of as a queen.

Sometimes I am still held by her fixed stare, the green eyes with flame in them. And the voice, harsh and threatening. "I don't know what's going to become of you. You're good for nothing. And you have no respect! No respect for me!"

I heard this speech or one like it over and over throughout my childhood — often after dinner or at bedtime. And I never knew exactly what I had done — maybe played a piece I hadn't practiced enough badly, or, without meaning to, torn a piece of music when I took it off the piano or broken something (once I chipped the head of Beethoven when I bumped against the shelf that held miniature busts of the musicians) or spilled a chocolate drink on a dress, maybe, that Louise had spent her hard earned money to have made.

After I crawled into bed I remember sobbing into my pillow. I didn't know exactly what had gone wrong, but I believed that I had to be better, that somehow, just by being in the world, I had turned my mother into a fury. (I didn't realize then that fury lived in her, that she had been furious for most of her life.)

"Yeah cry, yeah bawl!" she screamed at me.

I remember sobbing, "I'm sorry, I'm sorry," over and over, never sure exactly what to be sorry for, often asking, "Please make up." Or, "What did I do?"

But she wouldn't. Wouldn't make up and wouldn't answer my questions. Would stand over me glaring or cursing until I was finally glad when she left the room and I could cry alone. Cry 'til my throat ached and my chest hurt, the pain breaking, or seeming to break, something inside it. (Early on I knew what "heartbreak" meant.) Cry until finally I fell into a black dream.

(Before this happened, Robby often stood by my bed to comfort me. "She didn't mean it. Your mother didn't mean it. It's her nerves. She's worked to death.")

On some nights before Louise exploded, she appeared with a fly swatter and herded me into our bleak windowless bathroom with the ugly linoleum across its sloping floor. There she switched my legs while I danced and yelled, not so much because the fly swatter stung, as because my only parent who had brought me into the world and who I had considered my closest ally, dearest protector and friend, (and besides all that, a royal personage) now hated me. And caused me to hate myself.

"I'm going to switch you until you stop screaming," she told me. And finally I would stop, undress, hang my clothes in the closet, pull a gown from a drawer and over my head, climb into bed, sobbing so that no one could hear me, let the hurt out but silently. (That was an art, but I had learned how.)

By the time I was seven, I had learned not to ask my mother to "make up." After an evening when she lashed out at me, she didn't speak for days. When she did, it was as if she had no memory that anything had gone wrong between us. And I wouldn't have mentioned it because I lived in fear that the fury might come back again.

I knew that days for both she and Robby were hard, twelve to fourteen work hours in them. At the grammar school Louise often gave her first piano lesson before seven in the morning, and her last at the high school sometimes as late as five or even six o'clock. And all this time Robby worked in the store; he saw that I got off to school in the mornings and came out to speak to me when I came home after (I liked to play with my horned toads in a little shed he called "the store house" where I kept my collection and sometimes I stayed too long to practice much.) My piano lesson, which my mother gave me just before supper, seldom went well because as often as not, I hadn't prepared enough and because it was the last lesson of Louise's day.

So Texas falls and winters and springs were a trial sometimes, but I didn't hate them because, except in math and, oddly, art, I excelled in school, "A's" strung all over my report cards. I was the student chosen to lead group projects, participate in writing and speech competitions, and for the best part in the Christmas and Easter plays. I lost myself in these activities, and because I didn't know which Louise I would meet by the time I saw her, sometimes dreaded the end of a school day. But not of the school year. Not of returning to my grandfather, Uncle Lyman Roy and Aunt O, and the wild wood that to me was home.

Away from Texas and hard work, my mother and I relaxed into and took comfort from the Arkansas summer. Even grew easy with one another (as Louise said she had during a rare hour or two in summer with her own mother when she was a girl.) We needed the time she often told me just to "rest and talk." She porch sat for hours and I sat with her some of the time, listening and tracing patterns the clouds made across the sky.

My mother spoke, again and again of the family sorrows and of her life. "You are who I have," she often said, "to tell this to." And she told as if telling would save her life. I listened as if listening would save mine, often with a heavy heart, but also spellbound, no matter how familiar the story.

Chapter Fifteen
Louise

Daddy's Story

"Daddy when he was a teen-ager trained to ride race horses." One
summer day when we were porch sitting, Louise told me that.

"His ambition, they say, was to ride in the Kentucky Derby, but he doesn't
talk about that anymore. He's a little embarrassed that he had such an
ambition when he was a boy. He was never a betting man like Lyman Roy,
he just liked horses and speed. He never would learn to drive a car or go up
in a plane. Born too late for either, he said, too much of the old century in
him. His birthday, afterall, was in 1863.

"'But,' he told me, 'don't think I don't know what it is to move along. I
rode this horse called Fever and it was as if he had one when he ran.' He said
Fever burned up the track, all right.

"Daddy was the jockey on him at the county fair and the money he won
made it possible for him to marry Nella. And for them to strike out for the
south and west. He knew that country needed building. 'I knew how to do
that,' he told me. 'I had been apprenticed to a contractor before I was nine
years old. When I was too young to have sense, I thought for a while I might
burn the world up as a jockey.'

"He said he had done all right on Fever, and for a while was tempted
to go on racing. But that was before Nella's brother, Blaze, gave Daddy
permission to marry Nella. For a long time, Daddy thought Blaze was never
going to.

"He said Blaze had slapped Nella the first time he saw them together.
Daddy had walked her home from a spelling bee — he told me she was the
champion, (he was admiring because he had to drop out of school.) And in
front of her house, before he said goodbye, he took her hand. Blaze saw that
from the porch and when she came up the porch stairs, he struck her. Daddy
saw him do it and went up to the house to set him straight. 'Look here,' he
told him, 'I've just walked your little sister home. There's no cause for you to
treat her that way. Or to be riled.'

"But Blaze slammed the door in Daddy's face and it was weeks before
Daddy saw Blaze or Nella again. When he did — in the hardware store one
day — he asked Blaze if he could come to his house to speak with him.

"And Blaze nodded and grunted that he could. That was the only way
Daddy could have gotten to know Nella better — to come and call and talk

to Blaze — and tell him that his intention might be for marriage. (And that was hard for him to do. He had only talked with her at the schoolhouse — where he had been working on the building — once or twice.)

"For months he could only talk to Nella if he visited her in the house, in the parlor, and if Blaze was also present. He said he came to call some afternoons when she was quilting or sewing, (she was an expert with a needle as we all know.) Blaze would sit nearby reading the paper or building a fire.

"Daddy found out a long time later that when Nella was only twelve, Blaze came across her between the corn stalks being fondled by a neighbor boy. He threatened the boy with his life and when he got her home, whipped Nella with a razor strap so hard that it brought blood and left the strap marks for a long time on her back. And he never let her go outside, unless she was directly under his eye, again.

"Of course when Blaze found out Daddy was riding Fever, he vowed not to let Daddy in the parlor ever again. But changed his mind when he found out Daddy had won a big race and made some money.

"Daddy told me that by the time he did that he knew that no matter what her brother was or how fearful Nella was because of what had happened to her, he wanted her for his wife.

"There was something in her that touched him, I guess, and he saw that she was gifted. With hardly any instruction, she could make clothes and curtains and quilts the way he could build a bridge or a building or a house. And he saw there was a toughness to her — she had to be tough just to live with Blaze.

"Once he said to me, 'Louise, your mother was strong even when she was a girl, but there was also something soft and scared in her that stirred my heart. I didn't know what it was exactly, I only knew I wanted to protect whatever that was, that I wanted her near me. And that she was the one to strike out through the wilderness with.'

"Well, the woods waited for all of us. We were all of us meant for these woods and most of us, one way or another, have learned from them. Your granddaddy always said, 'These woods have been my greatest teacher.'

"Not Robby, of course. Robby never took to the out-of-doors until he went overseas. After he came back, we all saw a change in him. He did more and more yard work and when he had time (and he never had much) took to the South Texas beaches. He liked to jump the waves at Rockport. And at home he became a fine gardener — in that hell where we lived, he hid us all away in a garden. And he made that! In that barren refinery town took a special interest in planting flowers and trees."

Chapter Sixteen
Beatrice

Although our houses, especially their porches, were great places for story telling, when I was a young child I spent most of my time away from them back of the house, making my way up and down hills and through trees. From the time of my first journey to Iron Springs, I set out, alone and with others, on any kind of mission.

More often than not, I took the red road, which I came to think of as "the safe road." Many times in the summer I took it with Aunt O past the Village of Men into the briar and berry patch when she wanted berries and to the base of North Mountain when she wanted to pick greens. And also took it winters. Took it by myself once in a gloomy November when I went looking for the Wintershine my grandfather always spoke of and that I had encountered when I was six and lost in a circle of what I thought were the wrong trees where I had gone to claim the rocks I had found (clear quartz and some turquoise ones streaked with gold) and wanted to give as presents.

By this time I was nine and in the fourth grade. Louise and I had driven up to Arkansas from Texas for Thanksgiving and found our home country particularly dreary, dark and cold. (Robby was off in the war, and in a brighter place than we were, though we couldn't know that then.)

"I want to walk in the woods," I announced early on Thanksgiving morning and after putting on my new winter coat for the first time with its matching scarf and mittens, struck out. Grandpa said he would have gone with me, but the cook stove had to be fired with plenty of kindling and the fireplace needed logs and he had a pile of wood to chop. "Don't go far in he told me," and I promised not to.

I told him, as I had told my grandmother and my mother, that I would be back long before dinner. On holidays that was at about four o'clock in the afternoon. "I'll just take the red road," I told him. "And stay on the path past it for only a little way. I want to see the Wintershine."

He looked up over the woodpile, but said nothing, only blew out his breath out into the cold.

But after I left the road and set out on the trail that led to the base of North Mountain, I couldn't find it. (I nodded hello to Old Pete, whom I no longer feared, when I passed him.) The morning's frost was gone and the path, just dull. I didn't even seek rocks of any special interest, nothing worth picking up and taking home. (My grandfather told me later that many of the best ones were taken by those who ran the rock shops along the highways and in town.) Maybe I would have come across it if I had traveled further.

But the morning was overcast and I had promised to return early. And I remembered how frightened I had been when I was lost on this same path as a younger child.

I would be more cautious than I had been then. Never mind my rescue by the big light. Perhaps I had just dreamed it. Maybe I had been so cold that I fell asleep for a moment and saw it then. Or maybe a crystal had somehow sparked the shine. There probably weren't any crystals now, I reasoned, except in rock shops in town. But crystals or not, there should still be ground frost. Where was the Wintershine?

I had no time to wait for an answer. I had to return to the house as I had promised. I was old enough to help to set the table and to put the food in serving dishes. I would say grace, too; for sometime it had been my responsibility to do that.

But before the day was over I would also silently grieve.

2

Although the light from my beginning seemed gone, I didn't stay out of the woods. Once, years later — I must have been about twelve — I took the red road when I was visiting for the summer because once again I wanted to climb North Mountain as I had as a young child.

I was not too far along when I saw my old friend the spotted stray Grandpa and I had met on our very first trip together. The dog was getting along in years and moved at a more stately pace than he had then. I thought of him as a patroller of the road and a reassuring presence.

The walk past the Village of Men, and into the trees and finally into the clearing at the foot of North Mountain seemed to me shorter and less complicated than I remembered and the climb to the top of the old, worn mountain easy, more like a hike up a high hill than the long, hard pull I carried in my mind.

When I reached the top, I took the Thermos of lemonade and cheese sandwiches my grandmother had given me out of my backpack just as I had when I was small and made the trip with Grandpa, (the lunch was exactly the same.)

But this time I took my sketching pad and drawing pencils out, too. Although every teacher I had in school gave me poor grades in art — my pictures, which I often purposely made with overlapping colors, they said, broke the rules — I persisted in trying to make it. I didn't talk about this much and, as often as not, I kept my pictures secret and hid my pads and drawing pencils under sweaters and nightgowns in the chest of drawers in whatever room I slept in.

After I had eaten about half a sandwich, I sketched what I saw of the valley. Then I put a bridge over the river I found in it, and on the bridge, penciled in a figure that I meant to be my grandfather. Later, I made sketches of my mother on a far away hill (one I could see across the valley) as I imagined she had looked when she was a child riding wild Bob up a winding road. Afterwards, I did sketches of my Uncle Robby and of Uncle Roy and Aunt Ola – Robby, surrounded by clouds, a boy with a halo and white wings, rather than the shepherd he told me he had been in the Christmas play; (I always imagined him as an angel, maybe because in the pictures of him as a child, I saw that Nella had dressed him in white pinafores with big white collars); Roy, tall and thin, slumped over his drawing board or sitting in a straight chair reading out of a story book with a winged horse on the cover, Ola nearby, smiling and rolling out dough on a counter or sitting at a card table fitting a new piece into a picture puzzle, both of them suspended over the mountain valley like giant ghosts.

I tried then to make a drawing of my father, but I couldn't, couldn't even start. I had seen pictures of him and had been told stories about his life. But I had no memories.

The figures I drew had been projected for me across the open space of the valley spread out before me by the pictures in my mind. I needed the sight of the country; the people on my drawing pad grew out of it and the country gave them to me. But because I had no memory of him, it couldn't give me a single image of my father; maybe, I reasoned then, the valley I saw before me couldn't help me even if I had remembered, since my father had come from a different place.

Chapter Seventeen
Louise

"His mother's people were all East Coast," Louise told me, "the men
university educated, the girls sent to the New England Conservatory of
Music whether they were musical or not, (but several really were.) Your
father didn't play well, but he loved music, came backstage to talk with
me after he heard me in Oklahoma City, when I was on a bill there — he
had come to several performances in a row. His mother, you know, taught
piano and had a younger sister, a singer, who died of pneumonia in the New
England Conservatory when she was only nineteen.

"All of them loved books. Your father's mother chaired a literary club.
(She was, though, to tell you the truth, an awful snob. All of us seemed
to horrify her when she came out to the middle of the country for a visit.)
One of the brothers had his own publishing company and hired your father
as a Midwestern representative, and before he went with the company
to Arkansas and then to Texas, he had offices in Oklahoma City, though
I never knew too much about what he did. After we married, he had an
office in Little Rock, but I never went there. We never set up our own
housekeeping until he was transferred to Texas — he knew for some time
that the company planned to send him to San Antone. I just stayed out in
the country with Mother and Daddy and your father traveled back and forth
a lot of the time between Little Rock and Hot Springs. He wasn't a thing
like his mother, he was friendly to all kinds of people, and always kind to
everyone. He said he liked living in the southwest, liked the warmer climate
and liked the people — open as some of the places they came from he said
— and he admired their grit.

"But after the crash came, his uncle's publishing company went broke;
his whole family lost their investments and finally everything. His mother
who had been so spoiled by her family — her husband had been years older
and when he passed on left her well fixed — and who looked down her nose
at all of us down south, died in a charity hospital. That broke your father's
heart, but he had been brought up with a gold spoon and didn't know what
to do. He was just lost, and then he got sick. You got sick too, and I took you
home to the family — we had been living in San Antone. While we were
gone he got mixed up with a Mexican woman who nursed him, (she was a
nurse) and who gave him too many drugs and he stayed on them even after
he got better. If you want to know the truth, I think he finally just took too
many. If that happened I guess he would have had to be buried by the state.
After I went back to San Antone that last time I just never heard from him

any more and when I finally broke down and wrote to him — oh, months after — my letters were returned, marked, 'Not At This Address.'

"But you don't need to know about all that. In the beginning we had some happy times.

"When he came backstage that first night to introduce himself and to meet me — handsome as a movie star — I thought he was such a gentleman. And later all the family loved him. Your grandmother said he was the only real gentleman in the family since Dr. Artrum.

"I never told her that after Myria died, Dr. Artrum came to see me in Chicago. And more than just that one time when he came to tell me about Grandmother Melrose's death.

"He came with theater tickets and presents always, roses and chocolate candy and once with a gold bracelet he said would really show off when I was playing in a show. (And yes, it did!)

"I always thought he was a dashing man.

"But he was old enough to be my father, which is what I told him when I thought he was going a little too far.

"He slipped an arm around me when we left the theater where he'd taken me to a play. I admired him, yes, — but I didn't want his arm around me like that, didn't like the feel of it, and I pulled away and turned to face him. 'None of that,' I told him. Poor Bertrus Artrum, he just looked stricken. At that time, all I really had on my mind was making good with my career.

"In the years before the Crash, when I was in Chicago — oh all through my twenties (and I'd been here since I was eighteen) I studied piano with just the finest teachers — I was going to one day make a New York debut! And I paid for my lessons — and earned my living — by performing on the pipe organ at the Palace Theatre and a lot of the time I was the featured attraction, not the picture show, though I played for some big ones, almost all the shows Norma Shearer and Mary Pickford starred in. I loved the sound of those big theater organs and especially the Wurlitzer at the Palace where I performed for years and made $300 a week. Big money in those days I can tell you! I bought the best clothes and was always paying someone's hotel bill. Someone from the family was always in the Palmer House — your Uncle Robby a lot of the time and your grandma — and at my expense. But I was a fool then, glad to do it. Your grandmother loved to shop for materials in Chicago, your Uncle Robby with her. And I was glad to finally be able to do something I liked that she also approved.

"I can tell you that she approved my playing the organ in the Palace Theatre! Grandest theater, and finest organ in the Middle West.

"The first night I appeared on the stage of that theater that was going to make me a headliner I was keyed up, wound so tight I could hardly turn my head. (After the show was through, I found myself a good masseuse.) I was in knots when I seated myself at the organ and touched and heard it — truly rode it — and found myself swinging out before that crescent of stage lights, curved like a new moon, and sensed the breathing of the people, hundreds of them, on the other side. I'll swear I could hear them sucking in their breath. But I couldn't see them. I couldn't see anything for a while except blackness, but I heard the audience as if it was a single person release and then take in breath, and I thought of Annie Laurie, (and I hadn't thought of her in years.)

"And then I saw right before me — on top of the organ itself — those tiny people, that small golden-haired lady rising over them, her hair in golden ringlets all around her beautiful face. She was all in blue this time — periwinkle that crinkled a little when she moved, a taffeta I think. She did a dance step or two and smiled at me. And I relaxed, playing I knew as well as I ever had. And then she and all her troop were gone.

"After that when I swang out over that stage for an evening, or even an afternoon show, I always thought of her and wondered sometimes if I would ever see her again. Sometimes I thought I saw her shape rising over the stage lights. But until much later in my life, she never clearly came before me again.

"Well, of course, the talkies came in and when they did, I was finished in Chicago and had to leave.

"I did find work in Oklahoma City, a big theater there that still used an organist. And that was all right and paid well for a while, and that's where I met your father.

"I went out to the mezzanine between shows and was reading over a score there — swinging my foot, I guess, and my shoe flew off and hit him — your father, who was standing nearby — in his shin.

"The first time I laid eyes on him — and I can tell you he was a handsome man and, yes, more of a gentleman, even, that Bertrus Artrum — he was returning my silver slipper just like a prince in a fairy story. He told me how much he had enjoyed my music and a night or two later came back stage to talk with me and ask me out to supper after the show."

Chapter Eighteen
Beatrice

Louise told me she and my father were married only a few months after their first meeting and moved from Oklahoma where he had been a book representative for his uncle's company to Arkansas where an office in Little Rock was set up for him. Later on, just before the Crash, the company which was branching out all over the southwest, set him up in San Antone.

I heard the story of my mother's career as a theater organist in Chicago and Oklahoma City and her meeting with my father many times, and heard even more often about their awful end, about her perilous childbirth (after a number of pregnancies she didn't bring to term) her sickness and mine both before and after their move to Texas, and how finally, after my father's disappearance, Louise had to leave me in Arkansas with her family so she could teach music in South Texas where people still had the money for lessons and where Uncle Roy and my grandfather who built bridges all the way down the road called the "Hug the Coast" had literally paved the way.

I grew up with many mementos from my father's family; I looked often at his pictures — he was as my mother had told me good looking as a thirties film star. And when I was old enough, I read from the many books in our shelves from his and his mother's library. (I believe I was the only one in the family who read them.) Read Keats, read Milton — almost all of "Paradise Lost" before I was twelve — Shakespeare, too, the sonnets, and "Romeo and Juliet" and "A Midsummer Night's Dream" (I was the only student in my south Texas high school who, even before I entered had already read some of the plays.) Read novels, too — romantic stories all of them, (the kind I had always heard, so life to me seemed all romance) Edmund's own marked copy of "Treasure Island," and from a set of French classics that belonged to his mother, "Les Miserables," "The Lady of the Camellias" and "The Hunchback of Notre Dame."

And I looked at prints of wonderful paintings and read books about the painters whose pictures I came most to admire, Monet's landscapes, Rembrandt's faces and Tiepolo's figures defying gravity, his people all in the sky. I found several geographies, too, and pored over them, noticing that the boundaries of some countries and even the names of certain sections of the world were changed from the way I had learned them in school and wondering if they were different still when Robby had looked at the countries of the world in Fiona Lucas' big, blue book.

So I had all this, but for all the stories I heard about him and all the stories and pictures in his library that I thought might somehow conjure him, my father was less real to me than Louise's fairies. He had simply vanished into air and I had no memory. My mother, of course, for a while vanished, too, but through the three years when she was (mostly) gone, I could still hear her voice and hold a remembered impression of her in my mind.

The real people in my life were my grandfather and my uncles, and perhaps they took on extraordinary significance because my parents had disappeared and because of my isolation in Arkansas woods.

2

Together Aunt O and I spent many happy days. On one of them a year or two before I came as a twelve-year-old to sketch, Ola wanted to go through the woods to the clearing at the base of North Mountain for greens because she said Roy needed them. His drinking bouts by this time were few and far between, but they had taken their toll and he was still a heavy smoker of Bull Durham cigarettes, which he rolled himself. Aunt O said she was afraid his body was all but gone. But she thought if she could just get the right stuff into him it might begin to mend. "The body will heal itself," she said, "if you put good nourishment into it."

So it was that we set out into the woods to gather some wild greens, up Dread Hill — so named because every time we climbed it Aunt O said, "Oh, I dread to go up this hill, don't you?" — and down the other side, across the creek and up Pete's Hill planted with garlic and on to the red road where we saw my old friend, the hunting dog who wagged his tail and trotted along with us.

"Why, there's that dog," Aunt O said. "He has been on this road for years. I don't see how he lives."

"Maybe someone down that way takes care of him," I suggested, nodding toward the turn that led into woods.

"Pumpkin," Aunt O said, "not a soul lives down that way. It's just thicket."

We found polk greens, near the base of North Mountain as we had expected, picked bunches and bunches of them and stuffed two big flour sacks full, and when we were through sat down on a slab of rock that jutted out of the side of the mountain to eat the lunch we had brought along.

I loved these early summer expeditions with Aunt O (in July we would go farther on along the base trail of North Mountain to the berry patch), just two of us in deep woods. Aunt O told her best stories when we were alone together in this way, told them as if only she and I lived in the world.

"The first time I came here," she said, "it was with your Uncle Lyman Roy right after we married. We took long walks before dinner and it seemed to me when he first brought me, this was a place of blessing and release.

"Your grandmother Merrill never liked me, never wanted me around and this was a place we could get away. Once you know your grandmother told me straight out, 'Ola, my son might make something of his life if he had a different wife. He'll never amount to anything as long as he's married to you.'

"That hurt me, honey, and although she said this years ago, when I remember, hurts me still. Once things are said, they can't be unsaid. Anyway, it seems like your grandmother never got to like me any better. The family thinks that when I go over to Mother Merrill's for dinner that I don't hear her talking about me when my back is turned, but I do.

"'Lyman Roy drinks because of her, because he married beneath him.' It breaks my heart to hear that, but you know I don't think it is true. I don't think he drinks because of me.

"But, honey, your grandma can't help it and I don't take it personal."

Aunt Ola said no one ever loved Grandma enough or in time.

"Your granddaddy was too late," she told me. "Somebody made her feel bad about herself when she was just a child. She does her duty by Lyman Roy and she does her duty by Daddy and all her children, even your mama, but loving them is another thing."

Long after we had picked our greens and finished our lunch, Aunt O talked on and on. I heard how she had come to marry her Roy — my Uncle Lyman Roy — whom she met in Baton Rouge when he was there with my grandfather buying supplies for a bridge they were working on in East Texas — how she married him after only knowing him a few days. She had been married before, but she told me she had never loved the man. "When I met your Uncle Lyman I said to myself, 'Now here is somebody!' My first husband, he wasn't much good, honey. I married him when I was just a child, too young to know any better. But we had a little boy I loved so much who got run over. I thought I was never going to be able to get over that. I couldn't have more children, not that having a dozen children would have brought the one I lost back.

"But then I met Roy and he brought sunshine. He said I brought him sunshine, too, that the only other he ever thought of marrying was a girl named Hazel Cloud who was a moody thing, with something dark — covering the great blue sky — coming out of her. 'If I had married her I would have lived under a cloud, all right,' he told me. 'I'm glad I didn't, I'm glad I met you.' He wanted to marry me right away and said it was all right that I couldn't have a child — and he meant that. I don't believe, as much as he's grieved about other things, (and who can say what they all are) he has ever grieved over that."

By the time Ola finished talking, shadows had begun to fall and lengthened as we made our way out of the woods and onto the red road. We hadn't traveled down it far when we saw the spotted dog, which I thought of as a friend.

3

The next time I saw him I was twelve and on the way home from sketching as I have told you. He seemed to be guarding Old Pete's gate, stood tall and alert, ears up on just the other side.

"What are you doing here?" I asked him. Pete, as far as I could tell, was not around. Had I expected anyone to answer?

I don't know who I expected to meet or what I expected to see. Surely not what I thought I did see — at least for a moment.

A leaf lady — her loose garment made of what seemed to be leaves, white oak and sweet gum and others I didn't have names for, strung together somehow — an apparition through the trees on the other side of the road that I glimpsed for just a moment as my mother had the fairy people, the difference being that my mother told me she had seen fairies distinctly, clearly, and since she even described the fairy lady's garments — a pink one with shimmering buttons and a crinkly blue taffeta — I believed she really had.

What I saw was indistinct and fleeting. Had anything really been there? And had it been fleeing Old Pete's? Not want to be seen by him maybe? Taken vegetables from his garden? Maybe tomatoes and beans?

"Hello," I said, and as much to whoever I had glimpsed across the road as to my friend, the old patroller of it. Although he wagged his tail when he saw me and let me stroke his head, the moment I spoke, the dog turned, made his way across the road and disappeared into the very spot where I had seen someone (or something) in a gown of leaves.

My grandfather had told me about hermits who lived in the woods, but from what he said, they were such solitary, shy people (and he didn't think there could be more than one or two) that they lived far back in, mostly in thickets on the far side of North Mountain where we never traveled. That whole side of the mountain was remote and treacherous, he said, and mostly unexplored. He had only seen one of its inhabitants once or twice and the person he had seen had looked to be old, an old man.

Whoever, or whatever I had seen was up near the front of the woods, just off the red road near our property. Was I even sure about its gender? I wasn't. All I knew was that something with long gray-black hair had appeared — and only for an instant — in a leaf dress. And that our guardian of the red road seemed to have some connection to it or at least be on its trail.

Chapter Nineteen
Beatrice

After that day, all the figures I drew were covered in leaves. Although when I was six a giant prism of light that I called an angel led me to the stones I had been seeking (to give at Christmas), I was, unlike my mother, not given to visions. Except for the "angel" whatever I had caught sight of in a leaf gown was as close to an apparition as I had ever seen.

I thought about that a lot when I set out on expeditions, and in the fall and winter still half expected to see the Wintershine. And sometimes when it was especially cold, near freezing, I did, yes, see something of it, a blue light that rose spectacularly and grew brighter and clearer as it ascended off the frost.

Did I see shapes in it sometimes, or only dream them there? Wispy forms did sometimes seem to dance before me, but one quickly melded with another and I couldn't make out what they were.

When I was growing up, Louise repeated the story of the fairy lady she saw so clearly in the holly fields and again on the great pipe organ in the Palace Theater in Chicago where on the night of Louise's first performance she appeared as real as life. Louise had not one bit of doubt about what she saw and again and again recited the details of how the small, sparkly lady looked and what she wore. So evocative were her accounts that I could almost see the figure myself, tiny but shapely in her bright pink dress (or the crinkly blue one) and golden hair.

Throughout her long, sometimes tortured life, my mother from time to time either saw through the veil between planes of being, earthly and (perhaps) heavenly realms — or dreamed she saw through them. (When Louise passed ninety, the tiny lady after years absence, arrived in a white cap and a dress, Louise said, "the color of moonlit air.") She was frequently visited by departed family members, my grandfather after his death, and Roy warning Lloyd's fatal accident, and many years later in her old age, after his time had come, Robby in a white suit, on moonlit summer nights, Robby smiling and sometimes singing a song. "You see there at the foot of my bed," she told me. "That's where he came. Down there — " She pointed to a space at the end of the room. "That's my stage." Was this just imagination and dreams, or my great grandmother's legacy to her, the gift of second sight?

I wasn't sure, only knew that whatever it was, it had not been given to me. Except that once when I was a child and had found out where I was in the woods through the light of what I now suppose was a giant prism, (that is if I hadn't been so cold and frightened that I hallucinated the whole thing)

I wasn't, as far as I knew, aided by mysterious presences, never looked clearly into another dimension.

But I had seen something this time, something substantial and I drew that, whatever that was, over and over through those final summers in Arkansas before Robby moved my grandparents to Texas with him. And through my own high school years there. Drew it with pencils and crayons, even tried to capture whatever it was with watercolors and oils, (though line drawing, I soon discovered, was what came most naturally to me and gave me the best results.) I bought materials with money I made from the first summer job I had my junior year, typing accounts for a department store. I signed up for art classes at night through extension at Nueces County's junior college. And I became obsessed with picture making.

If I could only render what I had seen trembling in the world in the first light of my backwoods childhood, if I could only capture the postures, not only the figures and faces, but the spirit of my troubled kin, if I could only set down on drawing paper the mystery of the red road and the dog that patrolled it and make a shape, (more than a shape, a design), out of what had moved so mysteriously in leaves — if I could only do that, or just some of it, I might be free. Wasn't freedom as it equates with happiness what our journeys were all about? Didn't we hope we were journeying to a place of boundlessness to which we believed we belonged?

That was what I sought, surely, when in however inadequate a fashion, I began to formally study art. Even months after I had begun, I couldn't form my father's shape or face and I made plans to leave my mother's people and country so that I might learn how. And to learn about the other half of the family I came from, hidden from me as, the first time I glimpsed it, the wearer of leaves.

I began in the Hudson Valley and worked my way up the river and into the Adirondacks and then over into Vermont and after Vermont, down into Massachusetts. I attended schools where although I learned, I never made an easy friendship or felt a sense of belonging, and later held jobs and went on excursions in several states.

I liked the country, but couldn't seem to make connections, began to feel less than a real person there. Others defined me as a "Southern girl" which, I gathered meant pretty, but lazy and dim, or as a "Texas girl," pleasant and polite but hopeless as either a scholar or a person with an artistic gift. I often tried to please by playing the parts I was cast in, though I knew they diminished — and worse, distorted — who I really was.

Sometimes I believed if I concentrated on the landscape and really saw it, it might save me. The banks of the Hudson River, green in summer

— dozens of shades before summer came, gray-green to sharp, bright green to chartreuse — all with blue mountains as backdrop, blazing with color in autumn and white and beige or brown in winter — was the landscape in this new country that I loved the most, but even there where I discovered in schools and libraries the history of some of my father's folk (an odd mix of vaudevillians and aldermen, professors and preachers, and a singer or two), they didn't lead me to my father, or even tell me much more about him. He was still the big zero, bigger than that in Aunt O's name — not even a ghost, nothing so romantic or tangible as that, nothing that "haunts." Just a hole in the world, air.

And although I was now physically not with them, my thoughts went again and again to my mother's people whose names I hadn't found in libraries — courthouse records, yes, but whose history as far as I knew was mostly unrecorded, unsung.

More and more I was compelled to draw. And again and again I drew these pictures:

A girl, her wild hair flying, astride a wild horse.

A man, an architectural draftsman, crouched over a drawing board, making plans for a church that no one had commissioned him to build.

And, finally — sailing off a rooftop, then off the edge of the world! — a boy in flight.

A boy who grew up to be our Robin, my Uncle Robin. I was in college when the picture of him sailing off the tops of things, (rooftops, mountains, a long road that plunged into the sky) preyed upon me. For a time after his discharge and before he got on his feet, he was committed to the alcoholics' ward of a mental hospital, (he who had so often said, "I'll never be a drunk like my brothers.") Where had the fairies been when he was sent there? When at Christmas vacation I went to visit him in that bleak place, he told me more of his story.

Told me of the girl from the nymph ward who came to sleep with him at night. Of the Matador Ranch hand, Giff, who went after him in a brutal way when as a boy he lived in New Mexico. And finally of the girl in Hawaii where he first felt shackles fall from him, ("I first felt really free there," he told me, "though I could tell in California I was comin' loose.") the girl, Sharon, who reminded him of Fiona Lucas and was the girl with whom he fell in love.

Chapter Twenty
Robin

"'I liked the church plays, Robby.' Oh I remember how she said that. She told me how much she liked to go to the theater festivals in Edinburg. Her school went to performances there every year. She loved the Shakespeare. 'I loved the fairy plays, Robby,' she used to say, 'The Tempest' and 'Cymbaline' and 'A Midsummer Night's Dream.' She was shy as a girl, she said, but just had to be in a play and worked her courage up to audition and was accepted into the chorus of the Christmas theatrical. Then a year later she was a soloist and reader. And in the spring, after she tried out for the Shakespeare. 'Macbeth,' she told me. She got two witches speeches and the speech of the main Moving Bush. And liked doing the roles so much that she auditioned every year, and got more and more parts. But she told me she was mostly interested in the whole production, more interested than in any one part, so that by the time she was through school she directed the church plays.

"So many times I remember how she told me all of that. (And I guess you remember me telling you.) The way she said it, and the way she looked as she said it, twirling round and round in that faded dress — gray, but it had once been silver! — played over and over in my mind as I went over the books at the commissary, (my job was to manage it, just as in Ingleside it was my job to manage Cage's general store.) Well, one morning when I was finishing a cup of coffee and getting started for the day, this sailor came toward me with a flyer that asked for volunteers for an entertainment that would be put on by Navy wives and daughters from the Officers' Club.

"Maybe I had remembered Fiona for good reason. Maybe her spirit had been with me and sent me on my way.

"Anyhow, when I went to the Officers' Club for tryouts I saw her or thought I did, Sharon Marie. She was so small and pale she was hard, at first, to see. But she had an aura. She actually shone. And the light from her drew me toward her. 'My name is Robin,' I said. 'I've come to try out.'

"And she answered, 'You had better talk to my mother.'

"Her mother, I found out, Captain Scott's wife, was in charge. When I came in I had no idea what I was showing up for. A 'follies' the poster said, 'skits and songs and dances, scenes from musical shows.' I got there early so that only a few of the parts had been cast.

"Sharon Marie first asked me to read. I took a seat next to her at one of the tables in front of the small stage — used most of the time by musicians, a singer or two with maybe just a piano player and someone playing the clarinet or brushing the drums. 'Here,' she said (she had the softest voice, almost a whisper — she was so shy — but one that on stage would carry.) 'Will you help me? I need someone to feed me my lines.'

"The scene I read from had parts for children, including three or four boys who sang.

"I read the line of one of them. And she read another. And then I sang a little song. I didn't know the tune, so I just used an old one that Louise used to play. The words were in the script. And I didn't feel shy at all around Sharon — though she was shy, I think, (we were alike so I knew.) I was drawn to her from the first and didn't think twice about sitting across from her in a chair.

"'Oh, that's very good,' she said. And her serious little face broke into a smile. 'Sing that, why don't you, for my mother.'

"I hesitated. 'I don't know the real tune,' I told her.

"'But you are going to try out?'

"I nodded.

"A little while later I did, and Sharon watched me and because she was there I wasn't scared at all. But I didn't know if her mother or one of the other women in charge of casting liked me and if Sharon hadn't smiled and quietly said, 'You were very good,' I would have been discouraged on my walk back to the Navy store.

"The next day, Mrs. Scott, Sharon's mother, called and said, 'Robin Merrill, this is Meryle Scott. We all enjoyed the way you sang that song and hope you'll be in our show.'

"And that began a magical time. For the whole month of March I went to the Officers' Club every day for tryouts and rehearsals. Finally, Mrs. Scott chose me for three songs, one of them with Sharon Marie. 'That's going to need a lot of work,' she said the day she chose me, 'but we have three weeks to rehearse it. When you come back tomorrow I want you to know it without looking at the music.' And that night in my bunk I learned it and practiced, practiced in my head even after lights were out.

"But before I went back to do that, I asked Sharon if I could buy her some ice cream or a Coke. Privileges at the Officers' Club were new to me. I had just been promoted. I was glad to be out of a sailor suit, (I never felt a grown man in that, but always like a little boy.) But I wasn't yet used to my new ensign's uniform. I had never expected to be any kind of officer and was nervous sometimes.

"When she was offstage, Sharon shrunk into herself and wouldn't say much. But I did learn a few things about her.

"She was Captain Scott's youngest daughter — he had three and she wasn't in the follies just for fun. She had a love of musical theater and ambitions to stay in it, and years later I learned from one of the men I knew as a sailor who after the war went back to Hawaii that she regularly performed in the Children's Theater there, sometimes with one of the children who was her own. I knew she was at home on a stage from the first moment I heard her read her lines.

"And she told me about this that first afternoon as we sat in a booth in the Officers' Club, so new to me and me in my new uniform (it all felt strange), sharing a sandwich. I was suddenly embarrassed after our order came and didn't say much, but mostly concentrated on scraping the pimento cheese off the bread of my half and spooning it onto my plate. I don't know why. It was just something to do — I was that nervous! — (I told her I liked to eat it that way) while she told me a little about herself, all the while pushing back a strand of fine, brown hair, and sipped at her ginger ale float.

"When she told me about the way it lifted her up to perform music and how she had become crazy to do it all the time, I said it was all just new to me, but that I had been partially brought up by a musical sister and that I had felt at home on a stage in New Mexico when I had lived at a place called the Matador Ranch and that the woman who owned it coached me. Sharon reminded me of Fiona some way, but I didn't tell her that. Or that before I sang, 'The King of Love My Shepherd Is' in that old time Christmas play, I had been afraid of everything in the world.

"'I surprised myself by liking to sing in front of people.' That's what I did tell her. And she just beamed. 'I'm glad you did, Robin, or else you wouldn't have come to tryouts here yesterday.'

"After I paid our bill and left — I saw Sharon rejoin her mother on the stage where some were still rehearsing — I broke into a run. And when my hiking buddy saw me and yelled, 'Hey, Robin, where's the fire? Why are you in a run?' I answered, happy as I can ever remember being, 'Because I can't fly.'"

Chapter Twenty-One
Robin

"When she leaped across the stage as she sang, flying was exactly what Sharon Marie seemed to do. From watching her no audience would ever know she was timid. When we rehearsed that show, that was the happiest time of my life. Between rehearsals Sharon came to the Commissary often and on the Monday after the show was over I had one of those rare liberties and we drove to Makaynui and hiked up to the lighthouse. That's when we found the spot I told you about with the rainbow strung out across the beach.

"After we came down we went looking for it. I never knew if the beach we wound up on was the same one that reflected the rainbow, but if it wasn't it didn't matter. I was happy enough for any beach, or any place, to be the right one. We walked hand in hand, not talking, the water the color of jewels, emeralds in places, and in others, sapphires — clear and pure and warm and calm, almost as easy to swim in as a lake. We had suits on under our clothes and got out of them and into the water easy enough and afterwards just lay on the beach, our hands touching and looked at the sky with the clouds breaking in it. Then I turned toward Sharon, put my arms around her, drew her close, and she put her arms around me, too. I was a grown man, past thirty, and Sharon Marie was the first girl I made love to."

2

"Ever since that hired hand on the Matador Ranch who called me Geraldine and then accosted me — oh a long time ago when I was just a boy — I had been afraid to make a start.

"He did that, you know, that big he-man — "

Robby stopped his story then. And a long time passed before he worked up enough courage to tell me how that happened, it caused him such shame.

Giff, the hired hand, made Robby think he was sorry for making fun of him and told him he had something for him, a present, in one of the side barns, the one where they kept the horses that had to be broken, the one next to the ring. "I'm sorry I called you names," Giff told him.

"Come on in here, boy," he called out from the door of the barn when Robby had turned toward the house. "Come on in here, there's something I want to show you."

"Well," Robby said, "he showed me something, all right. Pulled me right into the place and shoved me in a dark corner. And threatened to kill me if I ever told anybody. And I never did. Not even your mother. He left the ranch after that and left no address. So, even if I had said something, no one could have asked him any questions."

Robby would never tell me, of course, exactly what happened. "All I could do was loathe him," — that's all he said. "And for a while, myself, too." I had to imagine the rest.

That big rawboned ranch hand forcing a boy against a wall, holding one hand over his mouth and pulling his pants down with another, pushing against him, and then into him. Whispering "I'll kill you if you tell anybody."

Robby, of course, wouldn't go into details of the assault, but he did tell me how he felt after.

"Oh I know what everybody thought when they called me 'Sissy,' that I was a queer boy. And yes, that sodomy, that rape, had happened to me though I didn't do a damned thing to bring it on. And though it tore me, I couldn't let on I was in pain. Stayed in bed as long as I could, treated myself with Vaseline. Tried to forget and couldn't. In my dreams even, it happened all over. More and more I wanted to stay away from men.

"Felt safe only with women. I hardly went out unless Mrs. Lucas or your mother was with me. I was afraid of my shadow. 'Robby,' Fiona Lucas often said. 'I don't know what has gotten into you, you're so skittish.' I jumped when I heard men's voices, didn't even want to ride my pony if Fiona didn't watch.

"But one day when I was riding in the ring, I saw her turn and go back toward the house — I think someone had called her, though I didn't hear. But after I saw her leave I took the pony into his stall pretty fast and had no more left his barn to pass by the next when I felt Giff's hands on my collar pulling me inside —

"An odd thing happened then. In no time he had me against the stallion's big stall (it took half the barn to contain him), the horse named Danger that was going to be hell to break — and the commotion riled him so that he began to stomp and neigh. When Giff let me go, I pulled the latch to Danger's gate and then I ran.

"And when I got in the house all out of breath and Fiona asked, 'Why, Robby, what is the matter?' I only said, 'Danger's loose!' And she was off.

"As things turned out, when Giff tried to lead Danger in, Danger stepped on him and broke his foot in several places. Fiona saw that it was attended to. But then told Giff to leave the ranch. 'You'll have to work someplace else,' she said. 'In a barn with unbroken horses I have to have somebody who has at least as much sense as they do.'

"I relaxed a little after I saw Giff go. But stayed away from the ranch hands and even from Daddy.

"I only wanted to be around the women, though Sharon Marie all those years later was the only one I ever loved.

"Not that I was a good lover. Sometimes when I remembered what Giff did, and what I heard Daddy doing to Mama, I couldn't make love at all. And, if you want to know the truth, only did a few times. But Sharon cared for me anyway and then it would be all right and I would come back to myself. I loved the way she felt against me and her breathy voice whispering, 'Robby,' and touching her skin and hair."

Chapter Twenty-Two
Beatrice

He meant to marry her, he said, to send for her after the war was over. Told her he would and told himself he would, too.

After he returned to Texas he wrote twice a week. Then Nella put her claim on him and he couldn't write as often as before. Finally, he wrote seldom, once every month or two, and one day he received Sharon's letter. A Navy man, an officer like her father, wanted to marry her. She hadn't known him long, didn't feel for him the way she had for Robby, but she liked him. He seemed a good man. She wanted marriage and a family. "Robby," she asked, "what should I do?"

His daring was gone. His family had too great a claim on him and from that blue place in the big geography, grander than any picture in one of Fiona's old books, where he had been loved and free, he was too far away.

Nevertheless, that is where I drew him. Drew him standing, sure-footed atop a high hill from which he wouldn't go tumbling off.

I started to make these pictures, before I even knew the story that went with them, the summer that I took off myself quite a lot in the woods. I was not yet in high school, Robby had not yet told me. I was maybe thirteen and only knew that Robby had been stationed in Hawaii when he was in the Navy and often talked of beautiful hilltop views of the blue sea.

And so on three large sheets of art paper I made line drawings of a man in a uniform on a hilltop with an ocean below, others of a girl on a wild horse, and still others of a fey creature covered with leaves. About two years had passed since I had gone alone into the woods and up North Mountain to sketch that first time and five or six years had gone by since I went with Aunt O for greens and saw the Leaf-Lady and the dog that had been traveling the road since I was a young child.

My uncle Lyman Roy had been sober for some of these years — I wasn't sure exactly when his drinking had stopped — I was in school in Texas in the winter and couldn't remember what summer of my Arkansas returns was the one in which he was sober throughout. It may have been one of the first ones, maybe even the one that followed the Christmas during which he had also been sober when I saw what I thought was an angel in the woods.

I was told that once when he was on his way home from a bender and a rainstorm came up — this was at the Spring Equinox — he was nearly struck by lightning, that lightning struck the oak at the bottom of the hill just as he was making his turn up it and missed him only by a few feet. No one was sure if there was a connection, but most agreed that Lyman Roy didn't drink much after that.

He still smoked and with long, freckled fingers yellowed from a lifetime of handling Bull Durham, still rolled his own cigarettes. The problems he had always had with his throat had grown worse and he sometimes saw a specialist in Little Rock. He still left home without saying much about where he was going or when he would be back, but no one worried anymore that he was heading for a bender or the track. Most of the time we believed he was on a job. Not that he often returned, Aunt O said, with much money, even after he had been gone for days, or, once or twice, for weeks.

I had just come down from North Mountain and was on the road heading home when I saw the dog, now maybe as old as I was and no longer trotting but walking at a good even pace along the familiar trail. I decided that for once I would stick with him and just as he was making his turn up it, said, "Fella, this time I'm going to stick with you." He turned off the road at the place where I knew the path wound down through some woods to the river, just across the road from Old Pete's gate where I had once seen him linger.

When I turned into the trees with him he seemed to quicken his pace. "Do you belong to someone," I asked, "who lives down by the river?" I knew of a house or two near the place where the water narrowed into a creek, (and on that road lived Maggie Fickle from whose place a dog I had as a young child had come.) But to get to those he would have to take a left at the river and keep on for another mile at least. He looked almost too worn out to do that. "I'm sticking by you," I said. "This time I'll see where you go."

We hadn't traveled the path long when we came to a clearing from which the river was in sight. The dog didn't go on toward it, but turned off into some trees to one side. I turned in with him and made my way as best I could through oaks and sweetgum and pine (and dark as it was in this thickness, the pine's bright green color leaped out at me.) "Where are you going?" I whispered, for it seemed to me, even then as we entered the mystery, that we might soon come upon a sacred place.

I saw another clearing then, came upon it all at once, this shadowed opening in thickest woods, completely surrounded by black oak trees; that is, their massive trunks were blackened with age and weather and the blackness seemed to extend even to their foliage. But some blue sky broke through the slender top branches and I looked up to the surprising sharp greenness of their leaves. The colors so bright it hurt almost to look at them. So I averted my eyes and looked down instead and then straight in front of me. Some yards away, I saw a tent, like the one Lloyd took with him on fishing trips, only older, it's khaki color more faded and worn, and in its opening, sitting in a pool of blue light, the color of the leaves directly overhead, a person covered with leaves (some almost blue in color) who wore a dress made of them. The Leaf-Lady I had called her, her face now turned toward the interior of the tent and away from me.

I didn't want to be discovered and the minute I saw who it was, removed myself from view, hiding behind a massive tree. The spotted dog went right to her, lay down beside her, wagged its tail. Behind my oak I crouched lower and lower, watched the Leaf-Lady turn to stroke the dog and when she lifted her face, I realized I was not looking at a lady at all, but at Lyman Roy!

Chapter Twenty-Three
Beatrice

When I saw him there in deepest woods wearing his leaf dress, Aunt O's
long ago Halloween wig on a nearby pole, I knew where he was all the times
he was gone and didn't bring back money. Sometimes in autumn he came
back with a bucket of nuts and in the summer with berries or a fish or two.
(In the dead of winter he never went far on jobs, Aunt O said. He either
worked for someone she knew in Hot Springs or he stayed home.)

I had his secret and couldn't tell it. Might never be able to tell and that
would be hard.

Aunt O had said to me, "I'll swear he gets more mysterious every year. He
used to speak to me about his jobs and who he was working for, especially
if he had to go off. Now he doesn't even leave an address." But she was so
happy to have him sober she didn't complain. "I do believe," she said, "that
he has quit for good."

And he had. Black coffee, buttermilk, Mountain Valley Water and
when Grandpa and I brought it to him, Iron Springs water was all he drank,
although when the throat trouble came back, it was hard for him to swallow
anything.

What did he do here in the woods, I wondered. And why did he wear the
disguise? Much as I wanted to ask, I knew I couldn't, couldn't let him know I
saw him, and though those at home worried about his absence, couldn't tell
them that he was all right. Couldn't give his hiding place away.

Ola worried that the jobs he took, which never paid much, sapped his
strength and often said, "He deserves something really good to come to him."

"Oh, Lord," I heard her say many times, "bring something good to him."

The very day after I saw Lyman Roy in the woods, but while he was still
gone, deep in the secret center of them, he got a call. And Aunt O told me
about the conversation.

Reverend Peabody, the Negro minister from The Church of the Morning
Star, called saying that some money had come in from up north from a
wealthy person in Chicago who had lived near the church and had been
a member, and that, with Lyman Roy's help, that money would give him
and his congregation a fine new home. They had long wanted to build one.
Lyman Roy knew that, had talked about it with him. "The building itself
ought to praise God," he said. "Mrs. Merrill, do you remember the day — oh
it was a long time ago — when Mr. Merrill showed me some plans he had
drawn up plans for a church that does that. Skylights in the ceiling so God
can easily come in! I liked that design."

Aunt O was so excited. She had run over to Nella and Roy's house to take the call (and I trailed behind) which had come to their phone since she had none and was out of breath when she first answered and never breathed easy while she was on it.

Lyman Roy would be back from some bridge work he was doing up north she told the Reverend and she felt sure he would want to take on this job. She told him that the church plans had been done for years (yes, she remembered the day the Reverend had come to look at them) and had always been special to him, his favorites. And that he always said just the very best Sunday singing came from Reverend Peabody's choir. And that just as soon as Uncle Roy came home he would let the Reverend know.

But when would that be? "Oh when will that be?" she asked as soon as she hung up. "I don't know how to reach him or even — and God forgive me for lying to the Reverend — where he has gone."

I did, of course, but held my tongue. And was glad I had learned young how to hold my emotions in.

But I don't know how long I could have gone on like this. Aunt O, I could see, was about to burst. Happy, but agitated, too. And as she spoke I could also see that Grandpa was concerned. "He shouldn't go off to work," he said, "without leaving an address."

"No," Aunt O said. "This time I'll speak to him about that. And this time I can. He'll be so happy when I tell him about the Reverend's call." I just hope he gets here in a day or two."

Lyman Roy had been gone three days and two nights. I wondered how he made out for food or if he, mostly, fasted. Maybe fasting was part of what he set out to do? I had never known him to leave for anywhere without a packed lunch. But even if he had left with one — I couldn't remember whether or not he had — how long could that last? Someone might see him if he left his place in the woods to go fishing in the river; he might, of course, snitch vegetables from Old Pete's, which wasn't far away. I had first glimpsed him there, and the spotted dog, too. Maybe, he just got along on very little; he probably took spring water with him.

I had read Sunday school stories about saints, and other people, too, who fasted — and I remembered a Scripture that said to pray in secret — but I never knew anyone who did. (People in the family talked about their prayers — or said them right out loud in front of everybody — and they all lived to eat.) Still, it would be like Lyman Roy to go to an extreme.

All this ran through my head as later in the afternoon I sat on Aunt O's couch sketching — a faceless figure in a leaf dress and a gray-black wig, a spotted dog lying beside him wagging his tail. Where would the dog go when Lyman Roy came home?

"You're quiet today, Pumpkin," Aunt O said. She had gone to the card table to continue her work on a giant jigsaw puzzle — she never grew tired of working these (as if her life weren't puzzle enough) and this time she was piecing together a map of the world! "What is it you are drawing?"

"Something I thought I saw when I went hiking in the woods — a person wearing a dress of leaves." Though I had drawn this figure many times, I had never spoken of it before.

Aunt O didn't think seeing such a person strange. "You see odd people in the woods sometimes," she told me. "Maybe one of those old veterans from the Village of Men made himself up a coat." She laughed. "They've been there for God only knows how long. They must have worn out the clothes they brought when they came." She picked up a big piece of blue, part of one of the oceans I thought, though I couldn't tell which one, and plunked it on her board. "Or maybe," she went on, "one of the hermits Daddy speaks of from the north side of the mountain crossed over to our side of the hill. They've got to be peculiar people."

"Maybe," I said, "but Aunt O, I thought I saw the spotted dog with whoever it was." I was growing bold and about to tell her more when I looked across the room out the window behind the place where she sat and saw the sky had turned black. And because I remembered being caught in the woods for a long time in a storm all those years ago (one of my earliest memories of the world) I thought of Lyman Roy with distress. "Oh Aunt O," I said, "look behind you out the window. A rain is coming up."

I had no sooner said this when both of us saw it fall. Then, as Aunt O snapped the window shut, watched the lightning crack across the sky and trembled at the sound of thunder.

"Looks bad," Aunt O said, "we'd better make a run for the cellar."

As things turned out Nella and Roy were also making their run for it, and the four of us entered together and stayed beneath the earth for what seemed like hours, but maybe was a short time. Grandpa told stories — one of riding when he was a boy through a lightning storm that brought hard rain. The horse, he said, was nearly crazy. "I had all I could do to keep him under control until we got to shelter." Finally, after he was finished with his telling, Grandpa walked up the steps and opened the door and looked out and said the storm had played itself out, that the rain was just a drizzle and that the lightning storm which had gone with it should be all but through.

When Aunt O and I got back to the little pineboard house we smelled
fish frying on the wood stove, and heard the grease pop from a skillet, and
then we saw Uncle Lyman Roy.

Chapter Twenty-Four
Beatrice

The months that followed were probably the happiest he had ever known. The church he had always wanted to build he was now, incredibly, commissioned to construct and became both architect and contractor on his favorite design. "Bea," he said, "it'll be a real temple." He didn't care what anyone else thought. Except for Ola no one in the family thought much about his new job of building, as Ola put it, "a bunch of poor colored people a church."

"A nigger church," Blanche snickered, after Nella told her. "Roy's job is building a nigger church!"

"Well," Nella said, "I guess they've a right to one and it brings money."

"He'll be the laughing stock of Garland County," Blanche said. "And he might even bring the family a visit from the Ku Klux Klan."

But Roy was simply happy. He marveled that in a country of dark, square, small-windowed houses it didn't seem to bother the congregation of The Church of the Morning Star that their place of worship would be large and round and flooded with light. The land where it was built was on a hill overlooking the south fork of Mill Creek Road (we lived on the north fork, but, as I have told you, from The Morning Star could always hear the singing); the congregation had gathered in a little frame house below the sight. "Now, we'll be able to see the firmament," Reverend Peabody said. "This is the very church I wanted us all to have!"

Not only had Lyman Roy's dream of building his temple come true, he was making some money, and though that only accounted for a little part of his happiness, he was glad to be able to buy some new clothes and wore good white shirts to work every day he wasn't directly involved in building, but was on the job. He bought a bunch of new clothes for Aunt O and me, too.

In the summer, I seldom wore anything but shorts and halter tops (the tops at Nella's insistence after I was ten years old, though she had given up sewing much for me. "What's the use?" she asked. "She won't put anything ladylike on.") Now I had a blue checked church dress with a jacket and a white shirt and riding pants. "Next Sunday," Uncle Lyman told me, "I'll take you to town to the Episcopal church and afterwards we'll sit on the side of Hot Springs Mountain and drink that good Mountain Valley water that they sell there and eat some popcorn to go with it and we'll talk about what kind of horse you might like to have."

This was the first time he had mentioned my having a horse (or anything about horses) in years.

2

"A light one," I told him without missing a beat, "or a red." I didn't know why I said that except that I had seen some pretty red horses grazing in a meadow up the road. "But where could I keep her? And when would I ride?" I knew the summer was nearly over and that soon I would be going back to Texas and school.

He told me I could keep her in a stable in Hot Springs. "You could ride her next year when you come back or even at Christmas if you come then. You'd have to have some lessons before you do."

I grew very excited in the weeks that followed. Wore my new shirt and riding pants that Lyman Roy had bought me to a horse farm that had a roan I admired. But when I asked about her, we discovered she was sold.

We'd come back to look some more we said. We needed to talk the situation over.

When we got home we decided that since the summer was nearly gone and that I had not seen a horse for sale that I really liked, I could wait until the next year to find one. I would save Uncle Roy the board. The red filly was the only horse I had come across at the farm that took my fancy, but, I told myself and Uncle Lyman Roy, the farm might get some new ones and, if I returned at Christmas, I could look again. That would be something to look forward to.

By Christmas Lyman Roy had undergone surgery on his throat and could no longer speak. I never had a chance to ask, though I meant to work up the courage to do it, what really went on when he went in disguise to that hidden spot in the woods.

He wrote notes to me when I went to see him and I wrote back, but I couldn't write a note about that.

"You'll be thirteen when you come back next summer," he scratched out on a piece of paper. "I may not be out on the hill then." ("Out on the hill" was the way we all referred to where we lived.) "We may have to wait to look for horses. Until we can, don't forget to visit the woods."

I hardly forgot, though I understood that my Uncle Lyman Roy thought that by summer I might feel too grown up to want to go. I went not only to visit the beloved country, but my old friend, the spotted dog, whom I suspected Lyman Roy had kept in food for years, though I couldn't figure out why the dog didn't follow him all the way home. He never passed Pete's gate as far as I knew. Maybe Roy had given him instruction to stay, or he was just too much of a woods dog to leave them. (Pete may have seen that he was fed.) I walked the red road to North Mountain and afterwards, walked the trails I knew he had taken into the woods from the road and I never could find him. The mystery went unsolved.

Lyman Roy died just before Easter. I was in school seven hundred miles away and didn't get to the funeral, though I wanted to go. The service was in a funeral home, not a church since there was none that he regularly went to, but the male singers, I was told, and there were four, all bass, were from The Church of the Morning Star.

Right after this, Ola went to live with some relatives in Louisiana and my grandparents sold their Arkansas property where they had lived for more than sixty years and moved in with Robin on the Texas coast. I went on through high school there, went East to college and by the time I returned to Arkansas, as a visitor when I was grown, the woods I had known as a child were gone, paved over by a superhighway.

I never saw the red road again, or the dog that patrolled it, but all my life I have traveled it often in my mind. Travel even as I sketch on a hilltop in Maui when I visit there, or a beach on the California coast.

Chapter Twenty-Five
Beatrice

My grandparents both died at home after they — and all of us — made a permanent move to Texas, my grandfather first — he was the older — though his succumbing took a long time. The sore on his face appeared shortly after we arrived.

We didn't associate it with his lifelong habit of pipe smoking, but thought it developed because of his diet, or maybe even because the water was bad. We immediately ordered Mountain Valley water to be delivered by the gallon. (By that time the water was well known and delivered over much of the southern United States.) Daddy seldom complained, so for a long time we didn't worry.

As for the others:

Robby, after release from the hospital, slowly adjusted. Married as he was to the store he came to manage, he eventually became buyer for it, seldom took vacations, and when he did, used them to visit the graves of departed family members, Lloyd, Lyman Roy and, finally, his mother.

Louise, who, except when she was girl on horseback, had never liked to travel, unexpectedly made a second try at marriage with a one time Ingleside refinery employee, a man with an ear for music who came to every recital in which she played. He became a safety engineer and when Louise met him again in Corpus Christi he had taken a job overseeing safety in the construction of dams. She traveled with him to the Northwest and when he died of heart failure after one of the dams blew up, she came back to Texas, moved in with Robby and opened a piano school. Until she came to live with me, (after Robby was dead) she never left her home country after that.

When she first arrived in California, a warmer than usual night in August — Robby whom she cared for through a long illness that followed his stroke had only been gone a month or two — the "fairy lady" as we called her, after years of absence, arrived in a white cap and a dress the color of the moon. She had come to soothe my mother's fears and make her welcome. Louise didn't tell me this, but I knew. Louise, I think was glad to see her, but she didn't let on.

Louise said, "She was sitting crooked — in a crooked way in my chair — that funny little thing with shiny hair. And I said to her, 'Why don't you straighten yourself out and sit up straight.' And then she was gone."

2

After college I worked for some years, less than happily, as a commercial artist for several ad agencies, one in Houston, one in New York, and, after too many years of this, finally went back to school, this time in familiar country, so that I could become a drawing teacher. I also married, a fine man, an American history prof I met on my first professional job in a small college in a Plains state. This is not the place to tell our story except to say he embraced the country in the manner of my grandfather (his own grandfathers were both immigrants, one from a small country in Eastern Europe that carried numbers of names and the other from Greece), and although life eventually parted us and took us separate ways, we lived harmoniously together through the better part of several decades, and with him I brought up a child, a second Beatrice; we gave her my name because it had been good to me.

From childhood I drew and I traveled and by mid-life, after I no longer lived with my husband and our Bea had grown up, took a teaching job in California. Certainly I had been conditioned for the move. Then, of course, like everyone who has been in Los Angeles for any time at all, I had to go to Hawaii. And the day I looked out of the plane's window over Diamond Head, I knew that the islands would draw me back to them again and again. But also that as a place that could put an emotional claim on me, they were a stopping place.

I had seen two of those I was in my early life closest to — my Uncle Robin and my mother — go flying out into the world (and in Robin's case, almost off it) — and one of the others, my Uncle Lyman Roy, withdraw into what was for him, the world's heart. Although now and again in my life I have, without thinking, in the manner of Louise and Robby, simply "flown off," I learned early from my Uncle Roy that withdrawal is good practice and that to do it in secret — if necessary, even in disguise — is important.

As for the "going off," it often shatters illusions, but (if we aren't also irreparably broken) we can, if we let ourselves, learn from the wreckage. When as a young woman I went east and didn't find my father, and only a little of his history, I came close to losing myself — I became so out of touch with who I was. But I did make some life discoveries that instructed me. I realized I was born outside the realm of the centers of power and that I always would be outside them. (And that in that placement there were certain advantages for the spirit.) Many of those I had cared about didn't fit inside either. Robin had always felt himself outside. My mother's talent found no outlet and for many years neither did Uncle Roy's.

Although when I was young I found my situation and those of my family baffling, frustrating — and, yes, humiliating — as years have gone on, I see it has also liberated me. I live now in Los Angeles, spend time when I can in Maui and Oahu, and every few years revisit Texas and the worn Ouachitas, little hills (hardly real mountains) where the woods I remember are gone. The church Lyman Roy built still stands, though (yes, the Klan tried but never succeeded in burning it down) and now is used as an annex for a country school — Morning Star — for black children and white, and shades in between. I don't know what happened to the old congregation of The Morning Star Church.

Woods and mountains do still live, of course, in my mind. And in the drawings I sometimes make of what I remember. And in Lyman Roy's book.

When he withdrew into that tent in the woods he wrote one and illustrated it with drawings more precise, more specific than any of my own. And when I looked at it I saw once again the red road, the Village of Men, the blackberry thicket, the trail up North Mountain, the place near the top of it where I went as a child with my grandfather to look out over the valley and later to sketch. And I also saw trails that led other ways, the one off the red road to Iron Springs and the one from a central path to Lyman Roy's hiding place. And the path to the river where, when he thought no one was around, he fished and swam.

In his book, under the pictures drawn with a fine pen, he had written meditations on all of us. Robby as flyer (once nearly off a mountain in the middle of the Pacific Ocean!) and singer. Louise as both pianist and rider. Grandpa as gardener, as woodsman (dwarfed by tall trees.) Ola, the worker of puzzles, smiling, piecing together oceans and continents. Nella cutting cloth from her own pattern, Nella stitching a dress. Then the surprise — for as a child I kept my drawings secret — me as a draftsman, and me who never really learned to ride, as a rider, off on a winged horse.

When I turned a page, I saw his entry on the church that before he died, Lyman Roy built and attended (the only white man ever invited to do so.) Across the top he had scrawled the words, "The Geography of the Sky." And then, this entry:

"When I looked up through the ceiling glass I saw as I had when I was drawing the plans, but more clearly, the way the sky was divided, the blue broken with floating cloud formations. I saw the sky and the way the clouds moved in it. I couldn't have seen them better if I had looked at spelling and a written message. The sky, the clouds, the movement all spoke of freedom, the soul's freedom — what in this scientific age could be called 'freedom of the mind.' 'Look,' it said, 'you are released! In your natural condition, the natural condition, each of us going our own way.' I knew then men had created artificial structures that lock us up and that I had been living in a prison.

"When I looked at the sky again and the movement, I saw sailing across that landscape, defying gravity, many bodies, some with faces, some even with eyes I could look into. I saw only a few at first — humans and other animals — and then, more and more. Overlapping the clouds and one another. Hundreds of them. Then thousands (maybe) — finally, uncountable. But all in their natural element, freely given. Happy — or so they seemed to me — "

I stopped there because I remembered Robby telling me about what he had heard, or seemed to have heard, as he stood on top of the lighthouse hill in Oahu and looked out at the blue sea. I closed Lyman Roy's book after I remembered. There was more but I thought probably nothing better, and I was too moved at that time to go on.

Afterwards, my pictures were of The Church of the Morning Star, and the sky as Lyman Roy must have viewed it, through skylights in the big, round room — clouds and humans and, as he had recounted, other animals (yes, a spotted dog) moving across it. As I worked on them, I remembered I had made some pictures like this before I read Uncle Roy's book. We had the same knowledge, he and I, Robby, too, once had it. (Maybe deep inside so does every living thing.)

Now when I look at the globe of the world and really see it, inspite of all the damage we have done to it, still green in places and in others deepest blue (blue and green blurring together finally), — an unbroken whole before me, a sphere — all the artificially imposed territorial lines are gone, and all the boundaries, too.

Chapter Twenty-Six
Beatrice

One day after I had read Uncle Lyman's journal, I had a vision, and, out of blackness, heard a voice. At first, blackness was all that was before me — a black void. Then a color formed a shape, a circle of deepest blue, blue with violet edges in the same hue as the violets that grew beside the flowerbeds I thought I remembered near the bassinet where I first slept. I knew that violet blue was the color of my father's eyes.

"I'm all right now," a voice that might have been his said. "Believe me, I've come through."

I wept for I knew that he was all right, and that I didn't have to look for him anymore. He had come to me, restored from whatever fate had taken him, snatched him away. I believed he would come back again.

2

I still think of the first long trip I ever took, my first "going out," that long hike through the woods to Iron Springs with my grandfather. (And the one before that in which I was helped by the Wintershine my grandfather had in my first years told me about.) More than half a century ago he gave me a sense of mission and set me on my course. I feel lucky to have been with him during his last conscious moments while he was here still on his, (maybe twenty-four hours before he took a last breath.)

He had cancer of the face. For several years we had seen the big sore spread all over one side of it. Finally, the doctor said he couldn't last, but for weeks he lingered in and out of consciousness. Before my mother and I arrived on the sunporch in the back of Robby's house in Corpus Christi, he had been out for days. We heard the death rattle from the yard.

But all at once, fully returned to us, he sat bolt upright in his bed and held me close. "I'm so glad to see you," he said.

A few moments later, I poured him a glass of Mountain Valley water from the gallon jug on its stand nearby.

"It's good," he told me. And then asked, "Do you see Lyman Roy?"

I shook my head.

"Well," he said, "he's sitting right here on the bed."

I was glad to hear that because, having given my grandfather water, I didn't think there was much more that any of us in the house that I could see could do. I held Grandpa's hand, but when he let it go, I knew Lyman Roy would have to take over.

Before this happened, Grandpa called out to my grandmother who was in another room (she met her own death five years later). "Nella, Roy's here." And when she appeared, asked, "Don't you see him?" She didn't answer.

As she bent over his bed, he kissed her on the cheek and then on the mouth, and after he released her, he reached for me again and held me to him. And then, even before I could offer a final drink of water, he fell back into his coma, glassy-eyed, unable to communicate and the death rattle began again.

3

Beatrice, Uncle Roy said, was for one who makes others happy (I haven't always done that, but who has? Who, even if it were possible, would always want to?) But "One," Aunt Ola said, "who is happy, too."

Before any of this, there was, I seem to remember, a harmony in me. Afterwards, like everyone who survives being named, I was into separation and trouble. But maybe by answering to "Bea," claiming it and through chronicling these stories, I have achieved peace of mind.

I am often inexplicably happy.

And this, in spite of the poison spilled into what I initially perceived as a mostly blue or blue and green world, the muddying of it, and in spite of all the killing and the fury and hate, and sickness, around (and sometimes in) me.

Is that because of Roy's naming? Or do I just have the gene?

They are all gone now — Uncle Lloyd early, my grandparents, Uncle Roy, and yes, Ola (who lived long after him), Uncle Robin, too, though, surprisingly he lasted well into his 80s — all except Louise, now regularly visited by what we call her "fairy troupe," and by the large light haired fairy-lady, always in her white cap, Louise says. Louise tells me that these days the lady's dress, like her hair, is almost white, too. Louise who now sometimes doesn't speak for whole days, still fully reports her visitations. Louise whose life spanned a century, now sees a new one in.

And I, as Louise's caregiver and family caretaker and recorder, I listen as Louise tells hers and her family's stories, and when she stops, listen to the others, all the voices that come back to me and on a good day, to Robby's singing in that soprano voice that I know belonged to him as a child.

"The King of Love my shepherd is." I hear him singing that and hear him say, as if he was telling Sharon Marie all over (or for the first time):

"Oh, you know — you know — I'm not afraid when I sing."

About the Author

Eve La Salle Caram is the author of four novels, *Dear Corpus Christi*, *Wintershine*, *Rena, A Late Journey* and *The Blue Geography*. She is also the editor of *Palm Readings, Stories From Southern California*, a multicultural anthology of stories by Southern California women. A member of Greenpeace who grew up in the Arkansas Ouachita foothills and on the South Texas Coast, she loves the outdoors.

For more than twenty years she has taught Fiction Writing in the Writers' Program, UCLA Extension and Literature and Writing at California State University, Northridge. She also currently teaches at Los Angles City College. Her books have been used as texts in literature and writing classes at universities and colleges in Southern California and in Texas. A short novel, *Looking for Johnny* and a collection of stories, *Eight Stories*, are forthcoming.